Hazel

Dearest Reader,

Camfield Novels of Love mark a very exciting era of my books with Jove. They have already published nearly two hundred of my titles since they became my first publisher in America, and now all my original paperback romances in the future will be published exclusively by them.

As you already know, Camfield Place in Hertfordshire is my home, which originally existed in 1275, but was rebuilt in 1867 by the grandfather of Beatrix Potter.

It was here in this lovely house, with the best view in the county, that she wrote *The Tale of Peter Rabbit*. Mr. McGregor's garden is exactly as she described it. The door in the wall that the fat little rabbit could not squeeze underneath and the goldfish pool where the white cat sat twitching its tail are still there.

I had Camfield Place blessed when I came here in 1950 and was so happy with my husband until he died, and now with my children and grandchildren, that I know the atmosphere is filled with love and we have all been very lucky.

It is easy here to write of love and I know you will enjoy the Camfield Novels of Love. Their plots are definitely exciting and the covers very romantic. They come to you, like all my books, with love.

Bless you,

Barbara Cartland

A NEW CAMFIELD NOVEL OF LOVE BY

BARBARA CARTLAND

An Adventure of Love

JOVE BOOKS, NEW YORK

AN ADVENTURE OF LOVE

A Jove Book/published by arrangement with
the author

PRINTING HISTORY
Jove edition/August 1988

ISBN: 0-515-09679-2

Jove Books are published by The Berkley Publishing Group,
200 Madison Avenue, New York, New York 10016.
The name "JOVE" and the "J" logo
are trademarks belonging to Jove Publications, Inc.

PRINTED IN THE UNITED STATES OF AMERICA

10 9 8 7 6 5 4 3 2 1

chapter one
1887

ZORINA was humming to herself as she walked through the Great Hall of Hampton Court Palace.

She was dreaming, as she always did, of the days when Cardinal Thomas Wolsey had first built the Palace and had been thrilled, as she was, by his wonderful fairy-tale building.

It was his favourite home.

He had his Palace in London, which was later to become part of the Palace of Whitehall, but his health was far from robust.

He suffered from dropsy and colic, and he found it impossible to settle comfortably in a house where he was troubled by the fogs and the chill damp air drifting up from the river.

His architect for the Palace was the Master-mason Henry Redman.

When it was finished and furnished with pictures, sculptures, cloth of gold and tapestries, it would have been impossible for any King to live in greater grandeur.

To Zorina every room and corner in the Palace was an enchantment, and she was so grateful that Queen Victoria had opened it to the public in 1838.

Otherwise she knew she would not have been able to wander about as she was doing now.

Undoubtedly the rooms that were not in use would have been locked and barred to anybody except the Royal Family or members of the Court.

As it was, she only had to walk from the Grace and Favour apartment in which she lived with her mother to the South-West wing of the North-West front.

Every day she managed to find time to wander into the State Rooms.

She was entranced by the Great Hall, which spoke to her of the triumphs and tragedies of English history.

She thought of the unhappy King Charles II, her favourite King.

He had loved Hampton Court, had paid long and protracted visits to the Palace, and collected wonderful pictures that were to embellish the Royal Collection.

He had loved, too, playing the childish games of Blind Man's Buff and Hunt the Slipper, and building houses out of playing-cards with the irresistibly beautiful Frances Stewart.

It was said that he loved her wildly and jealously.

He was broken-hearted when she refused his advances and later married the Duke of Richmond.

Zorina remembered the last line of the poem he had written about her in which he said:

"I think there is no hell like loving too well."

She walked on dreamily with no particular purpose, and was still thinking of the King as she entered the Cartoon Gallery.

Deep in her thoughts, she bumped into someone and saw it was a man who was standing just inside the door.

He was not gazing at the magnificent tapestries on the wall but was looking out of one of the long windows.

It was so surprising to find anyone there so early before the Palace was open to the public that Zorina gave a little cry.

"Pardon me," he said, "I was not aware that anybody else was about."

"They . . . should not be . . . not so . . . early!" Zorina replied a little incoherently.

Then, as she looked at him, she realised that he was not only extremely good-looking but also very well dressed.

She knew he must be a visitor.

He was probably staying with one of the many people who lived in the Grace and Favour apartments of the Palace.

"I am so . . . sorry," she said quickly. "It is . . . entirely my . . . fault. I was . . . dreaming, and not . . . looking where I was . . . going."

"Actually," he replied, and she realised he had a slight accent, and was therefore not English, "I thought when I saw you that you must be a ghost!"

Zorina laughed.

"People are always looking for the ghost, and in fact yesterday—"

She stopped.

She suddenly realised it was very reprehensible of her to be talking to a Gentleman to whom she had not been introduced.

She was sure that her mother would be extremely annoyed if she knew about it.

"I must . . . go," she said, feeling it was difficult to take her eyes from his face.

"How can you be so unkind as to leave me when I have not heard the end of the story?" he enquired. "I shall be curious until we meet again."

Zorina smiled.

"I think that is unlikely, but what I was going to say was that many people say they have seen the . . . apparition of Catherine Howard, who was Henry VIII's fifth wife."

The Gentleman raised his eye-brows, but he did not interrupt as Zorina went on:

"The story is that Queen Catherine escaped from the Palace room in which she was being held prisoner before she was removed to the Tower to be . . . beheaded."

She drew in her breath before she continued:

"She ran along the gallery to plead with the King, who was celebrating Mass in the Chapel."

"And did she reach him?" the Gentleman asked.

Zorina shook her head.

"No, she was chased and seized by the guards and carried back to her room."

Her voice softened.

"As the poor Queen was . . . dragged away . . . she gave a . . . piercing scream which was heard in many of the other rooms, and certainly in the Chapel, but the

King paid no attention and just continued with his prayers."

There was a little silence, then the Gentleman said:

"And you say that people have seen Queen Catherine?"

"I was just going to tell you that Jessie, who is the woman who comes to clean our apartment, has told me that a friend of hers who works here in the public rooms says she saw Queen Catherine two nights ago when it was growing dark and heard her scream."

Zorina shuddered as she added:

"I hope I . . . never hear . . . her."

"I am sure you never will," the Gentleman said. "You must see and hear only what is as beautiful as yourself."

Zorina stared at him in astonishment.

Nobody had ever spoken to her like that before.

But instead of feeling insulted by such presumption, as she thought later perhaps she should have been, she had merely felt shy and looked away.

She was pretending to look at the tapestries which covered the wall opposite them when he asked unexpectedly:

"What is your name?"

"Zorina."

She replied without thinking, then before she could realise how reprehensibly she was behaving, he said:

"And I am Rudolf! Now we are introduced, and I would like you to tell me all about this enchanted Palace."

Zorina smiled, and he saw she had a dimple on either side of her mouth.

"Is that how it seems to you? It has always to me

been too beautiful to be real, and if it vanished over-
night, I would not be in the least surprised!"

He laughed. Then he said:

"What is important is that you should not vanish with
it and perhaps become like the poor ghosts who cannot
leave the place where they were happy."

The way he spoke was so beguiling that Zorina threw
all caution to the winds.

She took Rudolf to the Queen's Gallery on the East
side of the Palace, which she told him was one of the
loveliest rooms she had ever seen and which she was
sure he would appreciate.

Then she hesitated and he asked, almost as if he read
her thoughts:

"Why are you worrying as to where you should take
me next?"

"I want . . . you to see . . . the King's Bedchamber . . .
but I think perhaps it is a . . . room into which . . . you
should . . . go alone."

She stumbled over the words, and the Gentleman
said quickly:

"I would be very disappointed if you did not show it
to me and, as the King is not there, surely it need not
embarrass us?"

Zorina laughed.

"Even though you are a foreigner," she said, "you
must be aware that we have no King at the moment."

His eyes were twinkling, and she knew he was teasing her when he said:

"If there were, would you be very impressed by
him?"

"I think I would have to judge him in comparison
with my two favourites, Charles II and George IV."

"Both Rakes!" the Gentleman expostulated. "Surely a strange choice for anyone so young and innocent?"

She felt he was mocking her, and said coldly:

"Charles II brought a new beauty to the Palace, sweeping away all the austerity of Cromwell."

She gave the Gentleman a defiant glance as she went on:

"George IV may have been, as you say, a Rake, but it is due to him that we possess so many fine pictures. He also reconstructed Buckingham Palace, which is, I believe, very, very impressive."

"You have not been there?" the Gentleman enquired.

"Not . . . yet," Zorina replied, "but I am very happy with what I think of as . . . my own Palace."

They had reached the King's Bedchamber while they were talking, and now her eyes seemed to light up as she said:

"Look at the ceiling."

The Gentleman raised his eyes from the crimson velvet hangings on the four-poster bed.

He understood immediately why the lovely girl standing beside him had thrown back her head to look at the exquisite allegorical painting by Antonio Verrio.

He thought she must have an affinity with the goddesses seated on a crescent moon, or flying across the sky with their attendant cupids.

He knew, almost as if she told him so, that they peopled Zorina's dreams.

They were part of the fairy-stories she told herself as she wandered round the Palace.

"Is it not lovely?" she asked.

"Lovely!" he agreed.

But his eyes were on her tip-tilted head, the line of

her thrown-back neck, and the movements of her long, thin fingers with which she was trying to express her feelings.

She gave a little sigh.

"Now I must . . . go, I am very . . . late!"

"Late? For what?"

"My German lesson."

"You are learning German?"

"I prefer to believe that it is Austrian, and while I speak it fluently, Mama insists that I should be perfect in almost every European language."

"That is surely being very ambitious!"

"It is not too difficult for me," Zorina said, "because my father was Greek."

"I knew there was something different about you!" the Gentleman exclaimed. "The English girls I have seen since I arrived in this country do not look like you."

He spoke as if he had solved the problem for himself.

Zorina wanted to ask him what his nationality was.

But he had not volunteered the information and she was afraid he would think it an impertinent question.

"I must . . . go," she said again.

"Before you do, will you promise me that you will meet me again to-morrow in the Great Hall?"

She looked at him in surprise, her eyes very wide, and he said hastily:

"There are so many things I want to know about the Palace which I feel no one can tell me as eloquently as you. Please, Zorina, do not be so unkind as to say 'No.'"

"But that is . . . what I . . . should . . . do."

"And do you always do what is expected of you?"

She gave him a little smile, and he enjoyed her dimples.

"I . . . I am afraid . . . not."

"Then do what I ask to-morrow morning! I shall be there, very early, waiting for you."

Still she hesitated, and he said:

"If you do not come, I shall be absolutely convinced that you are a ghost, and that I may have to search for a thousand years to find you again."

"Now you are being . . . ridiculous!" she laughed. "Very well, if it is possible . . . I will come, but if I have to do . . . something else, you must . . . understand."

"I shall never understand! I shall only be unhappy and frustrated and perhaps become a ghost myself, wandering through the rooms aimlessly crying: 'Zorina!'"

She laughed again, then she said:

"Now I am going to run very fast to where I should have been at least twenty minutes ago."

She would have moved away, but he put out his hand to take hers, saying:

"*Au revoir,* Zorina! If you are the Spirit of Hampton Court, you are more beautiful than any Queen or Princess who ever graced it!"

As he finished speaking, he bent his head and his lips touched the softness of her skin.

For a moment she was still, in sheer astonishment.

Then she was running from the King's Room and he could hear the sound of her footsteps fading away into the distance.

*   *   *

As she ran, Zorina asked herself how this could have happened, but at the same time, she had to admit it had been very exciting.

She had never seen anybody as handsome as the Gentleman called Rudolf and she wondered who he could be and with whom he was staying.

There were so many different households in the Palace that it was impossible for her to begin to guess in which one he was a guest.

It took her quite some time to reach the apartment in the South-West wing in the North-West front occupied by Baroness von Dremhiem.

The Baroness's husband had been a distant relative of the Prince Consort, which was why she had been accorded a Grace and Favour house.

She was an old but very intelligent woman and she lived alone.

She had, therefore, welcomed the suggestion from Zorina's mother that Zorina should improve her German.

Zorina had already learnt the grammar and the verbs, and what she called all the "boring part of the language," with a Governess.

But with the Baroness she conversed and they talked of the many parts of the world in which she had travelled and which Zorina found fascinating.

At the same time, she thought German an ugly language and much preferred French.

"That is something you certainly must not say to the Queen!" her mother had admonished her. "Do not forget that the Prince Consort came from Saxe-Coburg."

"I will not forget it, Mama, but we do not see the Queen often enough to worry whether she will ask me about my German lessons!"

Zorina was laughing at the idea, but her mother, Princess Louise, was serious.

"I am hoping, Dearest," she said, "that now that you are eighteen, Her Majesty will invite you to some of the parties which are given at Windsor Castle."

"I am sure that is unlikely, Mama," Zorina replied. "We are not important enough."

Princess Louise sighed, knowing that was true.

She had been very lucky in being given a Grace and Favour house after her husband's death.

Prince Paul, of the small Greek-speaking Kingdom of Parnassos, had been killed in an insurrection.

It had resulted in the Monarchy being overthrown, and what was left of the family exiled.

Princess Louise and her only child, Zorina, who was then twelve, had come back to England, more or less penniless, wondering who would befriend them.

The Princess's father, the Duke of Windermere, was by now dead, and her elder brother had succeeded to the title.

He had three sons and four daughters and was finding it difficult to keep up his estate in the Lake District.

Princess Louise had known he would find her an unwelcome encumbrance.

She had, therefore, been extremely grateful to the Queen for giving her and Zorina a small and not particularly attractive apartment at Hampton Court Palace.

It had, however, at least been a roof over their heads, and they managed to survive on the very small income Princess Louise received from the money her mother had left her when she died.

It was not enough for her or Zorina to afford many

clothes, to travel, barely in fact to move from their apartment.

She was determined, however, that her daughter who, like her father, was very intelligent, should have the best education possible.

That included more than anything else the ability to speak many languages.

Zorina, of course, was fluent in modern Greek and the languages with which she had been familiar as a child, especially Italian, Italy being the nearest country.

She had also some knowledge of Albanian and Serbian and the languages of other Balkan countries.

It was only when she had grown older that she had said to her mother:

"I feel, Mama, that the reason you are so insistent on my learning languages is that you are hoping that the Queen will find me a husband. I have been told Her Majesty is known as the 'Match-maker of Europe'!"

"Really, Zorina, you must not talk like that!" her mother replied sharply.

Then, after a moment's pause, she added:

"But, Dearest, you are right, and of course I am praying that you will find somebody as attractive and charming as Papa."

She sighed and went on:

"I want you to reign over a country which is as beautiful as Greece, and where you will be able to help the people, who will love and admire you."

Zorina had thought it sounded like one of her own fairy-tales, and she had the uncomfortable feeling that it could never come true.

It was obvious that the Queen, of whom everybody

was very frightened, was not at all impressed with either her mother or herself.

Occasionally Princess Louise was invited, as if it were a great concession, to luncheon at Windsor Castle.

But they were not included in the Christmas parties which were the highlight of the Season for every Royalty in the country.

They did not receive a Christmas present from the Queen, although they were sent a card, which went out to a great number of people.

That was all.

Although she did not say so to her mother since she was afraid it would hurt her feelings, Zorina thought to herself that she had no wish to be married to a man she did not love.

In turn, he would doubtless marry her because her father had been Royal and her mother English.

This for foreign countries entailed the support of the Union Jack and the blessing of the most powerful Queen in the world.

"I want to marry somebody I love and who loves me," she thought wistfully, and hoped that by some miracle it would happen.

At the same time, because it pleased her mother, she worked hard at her languages.

She knew that Princess Louise had scanned the names of those who had Grace and Favour houses to find someone like the Baroness.

She had found a Prince who came from Rumania. But Zorina found it difficult to make him discuss anything but sport.

Although she enjoyed being with him, for the simple reason that even if very old, he was a man.

It made a change from being with so many women.

Their own household was a very small one. There was her mother, herself, and Nanny, who had been with them since she was born.

Then there was Jessie, who came in to clean the floors every other day and was extremely garrulous, too much so, the Princess thought, except that she was cheaper than many of the women who worked in the Palace.

It was not surprising that Zorina had to rely on the stories she made up for amusement.

Everybody round her seemed very old, and there were no people of her own age.

Yet, she was, in fact, very happy, finding it interesting to watch the sight-seers who flooded into the Palace later in the day.

She would watch them wandering around wide-eyed and amused herself by trying to guess what they did and where they came from.

They were continually getting lost in the Maze, which was a great feature of the Palace gardens, and every visitor wanted to see it.

She knew even the attendants employed at the Palace would have wagers amongst themselves to see how quickly they could find their way to the middle.

At the moment the winning time was five minutes, but they discovered the way out took very much longer.

Zorina loved the Maze and she loved, too, to stand watching the barges and ships move up the river.

She told herself tales of what cargoes they conveyed and from what far-off countries they had been carried to London.

"One day," she decided, "I will travel. I will sail up

great rivers, climb high mountains, and ride through impenetrable forests!"

In her day-dream she was not alone.

There was always somebody with her, somebody with whom she laughed and who understood what a thrilling adventure it all was.

But the man who was her companion—and, of course, it was a man—had no face.

He was just there in her thoughts, a being whom she could not identify.

When she got home after her German lesson, she did not tell her mother about the strange encounter she had had with the Gentleman in the Cartoon Gallery.

She knew the Princess would be shocked, and it would have been impossible to explain why she had spent so long in talking to him.

"But he was very interested in what I had to show him," she excused herself.

She was well aware that her mother would have been horrified at her talking to a stranger, especially a man who was of their own class.

She had been instructing Zorina on correct procedure for a young woman who was to all intents a *débutante*, but Zorina had argued fiercely against this description.

"How can I be a *débutante*, Mama," she asked, "when I have not been invited to a single Ball and not been presented at a Drawing-Room?"

"I am going to talk to Her Majesty about that the very next time I see her," the Princess promised.

She did not, however, sound very hopeful.

Zorina told herself sensibly that the best thing she could do was to forget the whole idea.

At the same time, she looked back and remembered

the Dinner-parties and the Receptions her father and mother had given before the Revolution.

She wished she had been a little older and could have taken part in them.

She used to peep through the upstairs banisters at the guests, the women in their tiaras and beautiful gowns.

When her mother came to say good-night to her, she thought she looked like a Fairy Princess.

Now the diamonds had all been sold and the gowns her mother put on when they ate their supper together were very simple and something she had made herself.

Sometimes the Princess would receive pathetic letters from Greece from one of her old friends who was suffering because of the Revolution.

Then she would walk round the apartment saying:

"Is there nothing more we can sell so that we can help somebody who really needs it?"

"We need it too, Mama!" Zorina replied.

Her mother would not listen.

Her last small sable then was sold so that she could send the proceeds out to an old woman who was crippled.

It was then Zorina thought that no one in England appreciated how poor her mother was and how kind.

Walking back from the Baroness's apartment to their own, Zorina had wondered if she would see the Gentleman called Rudolf again.

But now there was just the usual crowd of sight-seers who were allowed to visit the Palace every day except Sundays.

Princess Louise had often been told by older people living in the other apartments that the idea of free admission to the public had produced out-raged protests from a great number of upper-class people.

They had been astonished and shocked.

How could their nineteen-year-old inexperienced Queen open a Royal Palace for those whom they referred to as "the lower orders"?

They predicted that the invaders would undoubtedly wreck the place, carry off anything that was movable, and generally behave like hooligans.

To everybody's surprise, however, the "lower orders," although they poured out of the streets of London in droves, behaved impeccably.

Some came on foot, others in dog-carts and pony-traps, and later in horse-drawn charabancs.

Before long the annual attendance for visitors was over eighty thousand.

This, the Princess was told, was a disappointment to all those who had voiced hysterically their forebodings that the "working-class families would behave abominably."

Instead, the Palace and its treasures gripped the visitors' imaginations.

Before long everybody was declaring that the Queen had been right, since Hampton Court had opened new horizons for those who really needed it.

"How could anyone not be better and finer for having seen something so beautiful?" Zorina asked herself a thousand times.

Now, as she walked back slowly because she wanted to savour everything around her, she wondered if Mr. Rudolf was thinking of the Palace, and perhaps a little about her.

'He cannot really expect me to come and meet him to-morrow morning,' she thought.

Yet she knew when she went to bed without telling her mother of her strange encounter in the Cartoon Gallery that she would rise earlier than usual.

Even if he was there, she would not have to apologise too profusely to the Prince.

The old man would be waiting to tell her about his horses in Rumania and the Castle he had owned before, for family reasons, he had been forced to exile himself in England.

She wished she had been brave enough to ask Mr. Rudolf what was his native language.

It would have been a challenge to talk to him, and perhaps surprise him with her knowledge of it.

But, she thought despairingly, it was very unlikely he would be waiting for her as he had said he would.

People said that sort of thing on the spur of the moment.

But when the time came, they had another appointment, they over-slept, or perhaps would no longer be interested.

She wanted to talk to him about the Great Hall, and how on special occasions King Henry VIII had entertained there.

She thought it would amuse him to learn that within the carved foliage of the hammer-beam roof there were the Royal Arms, in some places intertwined with those of Anne Boleyn.

Zorina had always felt very sorry for Anne Boleyn.

The King had been so angry and frustrated when her child was born a daughter instead of the longed-for son.

She had read in her history books that when Anne was taken to the Tower of London on a lot of trumped-up charges, she had begged one last favour of her cruel husband.

Could she, she had asked, be beheaded in the civilised French manner by a sword instead of an axe?

This King Henry had granted her, and on the 19th May, 1536, poor Anne was beheaded by a swordsman brought specially for the occasion from France.

Always when Zorina read about this it brought tears to her eyes.

She felt shocked and angry when she read that the same night the King had dined merrily with Jane Seymour.

And yet it was all a fascinating part of the Palace, and she wondered if Anne, like Queen Catherine, also haunted the rooms, although nobody asserted they had seen her.

She took a little extra trouble in arranging her hair the next morning.

She put on what she thought was one of her prettiest gowns, although there were not many to choose from.

She helped her mother to make her gowns.

She then wore them until they were either too tight for her, or else had been washed so often that the colour had faded.

The Princess was busy on another gown, but this, Zorina knew, was an evening-gown just in case she was asked to a party at Windsor Castle.

Or—more exciting—if the Queen allowed her to be presented at one of the Drawing-Rooms.

It had taken a great deal of their savings to afford the material, and Zorina knew despairingly that it meant there would be no luxuries and certainly no other additions to her wardrobe for a very long time.

The gown she put on now fitted very closely into her small waist, and the skirt was drawn back into a small and not very impressive bustle at the back.

It made her look, however, very young, and very lovely.

White was exactly the right colour for her when her hair in the sunshine shone with deep red tints that her mother always said came from her grandmother, who had been Hungarian.

Perhaps that same grandmother was responsible for the translucent purity of Zorina's skin.

She never sun-burned, even in the hottest days of the summer.

Her eyes were green, except in certain lights, but they had a strange, mysterious darkness about them if she was worried or unhappy.

At other times they had the clarity of a mountain stream.

They seemed to fill her small face, with its pointed chin and little straight Grecian nose, which she had inherited from her father.

Because she was so unselfconscious and had never been paid compliments except by the stranger she had met yesterday, Zorina had no idea that her mother would often look at her and sigh.

The Princess would be wondering what was to happen to her lovely child and if she would ever find happiness, when the Queen continued to ignore them.

There was nothing Zorina could do, meanwhile, but to go on learning from the old people who lived, as they did, on the charity of Her Majesty.

Zorina hurried along the corridors that led from their wing to the centre of the Palace and the Cartoon Room.

She was telling herself excitedly as she went that this was an adventure.

It was the first she had had for a very long time, and different from anything she had ever known before.

She was meeting Rudolf so that she could tell him about the Palace.

Surely, she told herself, to show consideration towards a foreigner and a visitor was only being kind, and even her mother could not be angry if she knew about it.

At the same time, Zorina thought it was better for her to remain in ignorance.

She went towards the Great Hall, with its high ceiling, and she planned how she would try to make him visualise the dais.

This had been set one step above floor level, lighted by the great bay window, where King Henry sat at a high table for his banquets.

Below him his guests would be seated at tables ranging round the walls. She could see them all so vividly in their magnificent brightly-coloured costumes.

She thought, too, she should take Mr. Rudolf to the Presence Chamber, where Cardinal Wolsey was the host at what was called "Minor Occasions."

She had found in reading the history of the Palace that it was not unusual for him to entertain hundreds of friends at a single meal.

In the Presence Chamber there had been scores of candles, their light reflected and magnified by the marvellous display of gold and silver plates decorating the banqueting table.

Zorina had learnt that the silver of a pair of great candlesticks had alone cost two hundred pounds.

'I know Mr. Rudolf will be interested in this,' she thought as she went over it in her mind.

She recalled how the Cardinal, half-way through the meal, would lift a golden bowl of hippocras, which was a wine flavoured with spices, to toast his important guests.

She was thinking so intently of what she ought to relate that as she walked in through the open door of the Cartoon Room and saw Mr. Rudolf waiting for her, she was instantly tongue-tied.

She could only stand, staring at him.

She had no idea that in the Spring sunshine coming through the windows, in her white gown and the flames of red in her hair, she looked like an apparition from another world.

For a moment it seemed as if he, too, were tongue-tied, then he moved swiftly towards her to take her hand in his.

"You have come!" he said. "I was so afraid you would forget me!"

"I . . . I am . . . here."

Zorina wondered why it was so difficult to say the words.

Because he was touching her, she had a strange feeling in her breast that had never been there before.

"You are even lovelier than I remember," he said in his deep voice. "I thought last night I must have been under a spell and that it was not possible that anybody alive and breathing could look like you."

"I . . . do not think you should . . . say things like that to me," Zorina stammered.

"Why not?"

"Because . . . they make . . . me feel . . . shy."

It was not only what he was saying, but he had not released her hand.

Although she tried to take it from him, he was holding it in both of his.

"I adore your shyness," he said, "and I had forgotten that when a woman blushes, it can be like the dawn coming up over the horizon."

Because of the way he spoke, Zorina felt a little quiver run through her.

"I . . . I want to tell . . . you about . . . the Cartoons."

"I just want to look at you!"

Now, because he knew she wished it, he released her hand, and they walked almost the length of the room without speaking.

For some reason she could not ascertain, it was no longer important to tell him about the Palace.

He was there, she had found him again, and it was difficult to think of anything else.

Only when they came to the door at the end did they both stop and look at each other.

Then Rudolf said:

"Show me, show me anything you like, as long as you stay with me! I want to hear your voice, I want to watch your eyes! I have thought of nothing else since you left me yesterday morning."

chapter two

ZORINA and Rudolf wandered through the Palace, and they were not talking of what was around them, but of themselves.

He paid her compliments which made her blush.

At the same time, she found herself unexpectedly telling him things about her life and how dull it was to be living with a lot of old people.

She also said that there was no one with whom to play games or go for long walks, as she would like to do.

They were just little things, and yet he seemed to be interested in what she had to say.

There were sometimes long silences between them, and yet she was very conscious of the fact that he was beside her.

At length they stopped in a window overlooking the

garden, and there seemed to be no reason to go on pretending that they were admiring the view.

"I ought to . . . leave you," Zorina said. "I am . . . sure I am . . . late!"

"I have the terrifying feeling," Rudolf replied, "that the sands are running out. I will lose you, and it will be impossible for me to find you again."

"I . . . I am always . . . here."

He hesitated and she thought he was going to say that he would not be.

She knew without his telling her so that he was going back to his own country.

She wanted to cry out at the idea, to beg him to stay a little longer, to meet her another morning, and yet another.

Then, because it was difficult to say any of these things, all she could murmur was:

"There is . . . a lot more of the . . . Palace you have not . . . yet seen, and there is the garden . . . and the Maze."

She knew it would be difficult to take him into the garden without there being eyes at the windows.

Someone would be sure to report to her mother that she was accompanied by a handsome young man.

Yet, she had a sudden yearning to hold on to him, to keep him from going away from her.

Then, as she looked up into his eyes, they were both very still.

"I feel that I have known you since the beginning of eternity," he said in a low voice, "and that everything we do and everything we say we have done before."

"I . . . I feel the . . . same," Zorina whispered.

He reached out to take her hand.

"We have to talk about this," he said. "Will you meet me again this afternoon?"

"It would be impossible," Zorina said quickly. "I am not supposed to come into the Palace when the public are here."

"Then suppose I call at your apartment?"

"No, no! That would be a . . . mistake! We would have to . . . explain that we have not been . . . properly . . . introduced."

"Except by the ghost of Cardinal Wolsey!"

Zorina laughed.

Then, because she wanted so much to stay and yet she knew she must go, she took her hand from his.

"I . . . I will . . . see you to-morrow."

The words were little more than a whisper, but he heard them.

"I will be here! You know I will be here!" he said. "In these few minutes we are together it is so frustrating, so infuriating."

He paused before he said, and his voice seemed to deepen:

"I want to talk to you for a long time. I want to tell you about myself, and learn about you."

Zorina made a little murmur. Then he said:

"I have an idea—I will call on you, informally first, and it seems a ridiculous question when we already know each other so well, but you must tell me your full name."

Zorina was frightened.

If he knew who she was, and the people with whom he was staying knew they had met in this strange manner, she was certain they would gossip about it to the other inhabitants at the Palace.

Then, undoubtedly, the whole story would be related to her mother.

It flashed through her mind that not only would her mother be angry, but everybody else would think it extremely "fast" of her to talk to a strange man.

Worse still, she had met him by appointment, and allowed him to call her by her Christian name.

Because she was frightened, she turned away from him, saying:

"I must go . . . I must go . . . but I will be here tomorrow . . . then . . . perhaps I can explain . . ."

Her voice trailed away, as she was already half-way towards the door.

Before he had really realised she was leaving, or could catch up with her, she was gone.

He knew she would be running swiftly down the long corridors which led to the Grace and Favour apartment.

He turned back to the window, but now he did not see the sunlit garden.

There was a frown between his eyes as he stared into his own future.

* * *

Zorina was breathless by the time she reached the Prince's apartment.

Then she slowed her pace a little and put her hands up to her hair to tidy it.

She was aware that the door was open and there was somebody just inside it.

With an effort, she forced herself to walk a little more circumspectly.

Then, to her astonishment, she saw Nanny standing there in the small hall talking to the Prince's personal

27

servant, who was almost as old as he was.

When she saw Zorina come through the door, Nanny made a sound that was half an exclamation and half a sound of rebuke.

"Where have you been, Your Royal Highness?" she asked sharply. "I have been waiting here long enough for you to walk round the whole Palace instead of coming straight to this apartment, as you should have done!"

"I . . . I am sorry, Nanny," Zorina said, "but . . . why are you here?"

"You are to come back with me at once!" Nanny replied. "And waste no more time."

"But . . . why?"

"I'll tell you about it on the way."

Her manner, when she spoke, made Zorina aware that she did not wish to speak in front of the Prince's servant.

Zorina therefore said:

"Good-morning, Hans! Will you tell His Highness how sad I am that I will not be able to have my conversation with him this morning?"

"I tell him, Your Highness, an' I know he'll be disappointed."

"Come along! Come along!" Zorina heard Nanny murmuring.

She was already outside in the corridor, and Zorina paused only to say:

"Tell His Highness I will come to-morrow, if it is possible."

The servant bowed and without waiting for his reply Zorina hurried after Nanny, who was already moving down the corridor.

"What is it? What has happened?" Zorina asked as she reached her.

"A messenger arrived from Windsor Castle just after you'd left."

"From Windsor Castle?" Zorina exclaimed.

"Yes," Nanny replied, "and Her Royal Highness's extremely annoyed that you'd left so early without telling her that you were going."

"I did . . . not wish to . . . disturb Mama," Zorina said lamely.

Nanny did not speak, and Zorina knew that she was finding the pace at which they were moving did not enable her to converse at the same time.

Zorina could therefore only wonder what had happened and what was the message that had arrived from Windsor Castle.

She thought that whatever it was, it would make her mother agitated.

If they were to visit the Queen, there would be gowns to be pressed and bonnets to be refurbished.

'We will look very dowdy,' she thought.

All the available money they had would not be enough to buy anything new after they had spent so much on the evening-gown in which her mother hoped she might be presented.

It took Zorina and Nanny quite a little time to reach their own apartment, and it necessitated going down one staircase and up another, so Nanny was quite breathless when they arrived.

The door was open and they walked in.

Zorina went straight to the Sitting-Room, where she was sure her mother would be waiting for her, and she was not mistaken.

Princess Louise was sitting in the window, sewing fresh ribbons onto a bonnet.

She looked up as Zorina entered and exclaimed:

"Oh, there you are, Zorina! How could you have gone away just when I wanted you?"

"What has happened, Mama?"

"Sit down, Dearest, I have a lot to tell you."

Zorina did as she was told, sitting on a chair next to her mother and looking at her with questioning eyes.

"One of Her Majesty's *Aides-de-Camp* arrived while I was having breakfast," Princess Louise began. "He was a charming man and told me that when he was young he had met your father."

From the way her mother spoke Zorina knew this had been a memorable moment.

Princess Louise had always been conscious that the few people they did know in England were not in the least impressed by Prince Paul.

In fact, the majority had no idea that he had ever existed.

They had heard of his father the King, but because Paul was a younger son, he was of no importance, nor, for that matter, were what remained of his family.

There was a little pause after the Princess had spoken. Then, because Zorina was curious, she asked:

"Why did he come here, Mama? It could not have been just to talk about Papa."

"No, of course not," the Princess agreed. "He came to tell me, my Dearest, that the Queen has invited us to dine at Windsor Castle and to stay the night."

"To stay the night?" Zorina exclaimed. "But, Mama, how exciting! It is something we have never done before!"

"This is a very special occasion, and I understand that the Queen wishes to speak to you as soon as we arrive."

There was something in the way her mother spoke that made Zorina ask nervously:

"Why . . . do you think she . . . wants to speak to me Mama?"

"I think," Princess Louise answered, "in fact I am sure from what the *Aide-de-Camp* said, that the Queen is planning your marriage."

"M-my . . . marriage?" Zorina repeated. "But . . . I have not yet . . . been presented! I have never before even been to a party at Windsor Castle!"

"I know," the Princess answered, "but now you are eighteen!"

Zorina got to her feet.

"I am sure you . . . must be wrong, Mama! I cannot believe . . . that the Queen would want me to be . . . married when I have not yet been to . . . any social functions or met . . . anyone except for the . . . old people in the Palace."

"Dearest, we must not be critical," Princess Louise said. "If there is some escape for you from what I know is a very dull life, then I shall know that my prayers have been answered!"

"B-but . . . I do not . . . want to be married, Mama! At least, not so . . . quickly!"

"It may be something quite different," the Princess said soothingly. "It is just what I thought myself would happen, and although, of course, the messenger from the Queen was extremely discreet, I had the feeling that was what was in his mind."

Zorina stood at the window, but instead of feeling

an excitement at what lay ahead, she was thinking of Rudolf.

He would be waiting for her, as she had promised she would meet him to-morrow morning, but she would not be there.

Too late she wished she had asked him with whom he was staying, so that at least she could have sent him a message.

"Why did I not tell him who I was?" she asked herself.

She knew the answer was quite simple: they were so absorbed in their talk about what they thought and what they felt that anything else seemed to fade into insignificance.

They had been together, and every word they exchanged seemed to have a kind of magic about it.

"Now we have a great deal to do," the Princess was saying. "Thank goodness I finished your evening-gown yesterday! There are still a few things to be done to it, but you can wear it to-night."

Zorina did not speak, and her mother went on:

"I am afraid you have nothing new in which to travel, except for your Sunday best, which is a little shabby, but I have furbished up your bonnet."

She paused for breath before she said:

"Now you had better go and pack everything else you think you will need. See that your shoes are clean, and that you have enough handkerchiefs!"

Still Zorina did not answer, and after a moment the Princess said sharply:

"Come along, Zorina! Have you listened to what I said?"

"Y-yes . . . of course, Mama."

"Then hurry, hurry! We must have a very early luncheon because the carriage will be here at twelve-thirty."

"The Queen is sending a carriage for us?"

"Of course, Dearest! She knows we have no other means of reaching her, except by hiring horses, which it would be impossible for us to afford."

"I will . . . go and . . . pack."

Zorina had reached the door before the Princess, who was gathering up her sewing-basket, said:

"It is very exciting, is it not? And now you will be able to see the Dining-Hall when the table is laid and the candelabra are all lit."

"Yes . . . Mama."

Even to herself Zorina thought her voice sounded dull.

She knew she ought to show more excitement or it would hurt her mother.

At the same time, she could not help feeling how disappointed Rudolf would be when he waited in vain for her to-morrow morning.

He would not understand that she could not come even though she wanted to!

She packed all the things that Nanny had pressed for her, also a great many others which she thought it unlikely she would want, but both her mother and Nanny were insistent she should take with her.

Finally the white gown, with its beautifully draped skirt and little cascades of frills down the back which formed both the bustle and the train, was placed almost reverently on top of the trunk.

Nanny was fussing in case it should be crushed and

there would be no time to press it when they reached Windsor Castle.

"We should be there by three o'clock," the Princess said reassuringly.

"Irons take time to heat!" Nanny retorted unnecessarily.

The luncheon was a very frugal meal eaten hurriedly with a lot of last-minute questions as to what might have been forgotten.

They drove off in a very comfortable carriage with the Royal insignia on the carriage doors and the top-hatted coachman and footman wearing the Royal livery.

The horses moved fast and Zorina enjoyed looking out of the windows.

They passed through villages which, although she had lived so near them for six years, she had never seen before.

At last they saw the Castle ahead with the Queen's standard flying against the sky.

Zorina felt with a little constriction of her heart that this was a very important moment for her.

At the same time, it was frightening.

She was afraid of the Queen, afraid for her future, afraid of being propelled, as it were, into a whirl-pool from which there was no escape.

"Now, do remember, Zorina," her mother admonished her as the horses climbed the hill towards the Castle gates, "to the Queen you are 'Victoria,' and you were in fact Christened after her because your grandfather admired her so tremendously."

"I expect, if the truth were told, Mama, he admired England, as do all the other countries of Europe."

"That is not the sort of thing you should say," the

Princess retorted, "and everybody in the world admires and respects Queen Victoria!"

"I have heard that people grumble a great deal because she incarcerates herself in the Castle and never goes to London!" Zorina remarked.

The Princess sighed.

"If you are going to be argumentative, I shall be sorry that we have come!"

"You are not in the least sorry, Mama." Zorina smiled. "You are much more excited than I am, and perhaps we will find it is you that the Queen has a husband for!"

"Zorina! You will give me a heart-attack!" the Princess exclaimed.

Zorina knew her mother was only pretending to be shocked because Nanny was with them.

She was accompanying them as a "lady's-maid" since, of course, the Princess did not have one.

She was as used as her mistress was to the provocative remarks Zorina made and at which they both laughed when they were at home.

Zorina knew now that her mother was nervous, and she slipped her hand into hers as she said:

"Do not be frightened of the Queen, Mama. I am sure Papa, if he were alive, would have stood up to her!"

"It is not a question of 'standing up' to her, Zorina," her mother replied, "it is just that we are completely dependent upon her, and should be very grateful."

"Well . . . she has certainly given us somewhere to live," Zorina remarked, "but she has not done much else. After all, Mama, even if I were too young to attend her parties, she might have asked you!"

Because the Princess had often thought the same thing, she did not answer.

Her grandmother had been a distant relative of the Royal Family, which was why she had been allowed to marry Prince Paul when he fell in love with her.

But she had never been accorded the attention that was her right.

She was, after all, the daughter-in-law of a King and the daughter of an English Duke whose mother had been a relative of the Queen.

"All that matters," Nanny said briskly, "is that we're here now, and you both, and that goes for you, Your Royal Highness, might as well enjoy yourselves in case you're never asked again!"

It was the sort of thing that Nanny would say, and both the Princess and Zorina laughed, which seemed to break the tension.

They drew up at the door of the Castle to find a red carpet had been run down the steps, and there was what seemed to Zorina to be an army of servants in Royal livery waiting to receive them.

Her mother was still smiling as they walked quite a long way to the private apartments.

Zorina was thinking as she did so that the Castle was more austere and in no way as attractive as Hampton Court Palace.

She had been at Windsor Castle once before soon after she and her mother had arrived in England.

Both had been in heavy mourning, and deeply distressed at the death of Prince Paul.

It was difficult then for Zorina to think of anything but her mother's unhappiness and also her own, for she had been extremely fond of her father.

Now she tried to take in every detail of the Castle.

After they had been greeted by a Lady-in-Waiting, they were finally shown to their bed-rooms.

There they could wash and tidy themselves before being seen by the Queen, but Zorina was not as impressed as she should have been.

She found herself wondering what Rudolf would have thought of the Castle.

She wished they could look over it together.

At last, when she had washed her face and hands and Nanny had tidied her hair, Zorina went to her mother's room, which was next door, to see if she was ready.

"I suppose really," the Princess said as she entered, "we are expected to change after that long drive, but your gown looks very attractive, Dearest, and is hardly creased."

"It is the best I have, Mama," Zorina said. "If the Queen does not like it, she can always give me another one!"

The Princess gave a little cry and put her fingers to her lips.

"For goodness' sake, Zorina, be careful what you say! I am sure even the walls have ears, and the Queen would definitely not be amused by a remark like that!"

"I am not likely to say it to the Queen!" Zorina replied. "Do not look so worried, Mama! Just remember that Papa thought you were the most beautiful person he had ever seen in his life, and our faces are far more important than the clothes we have on our rather ordinary bodies."

The Princess laughed, as her daughter meant her to do.

"You are incorrigible, Zorina!" she exclaimed. "I cannot think what I can do to you!"

"Just let me be myself, Mama," Zorina said, "and let us enjoy the first visit we have paid here in six years, and eat everything that is put in front of us!"

The Princess laughed again.

She walked from the bed-room towards the Sitting-Room, where she knew there would be somebody waiting for them.

Zorina was thinking that however many critical people there might be at Court, no one could look more regal or more lovely than her mother.

It was true that Prince Paul had fallen in love with her the first time he saw her.

It was in a tent at Royal Ascot, to which he had been invited to luncheon by the Duke of Windermere.

He had gone to the races because he was interested in the horses, but the moment he saw Lady Louise, he had found it impossible to think of anything but her.

He had not lost his money but his heart.

Because he was Royal, if only the younger son of King Minos, he was of certain importance, and he and Louise had been terrified that they would not have permission to marry.

Fortunately for them, King Minos had too many political problems on his hands to be very much concerned with any family difficulties.

At the time, Queen Victoria was so deeply in love with Prince Albert that she was sympathetic and understanding when other people were in love.

She therefore agreed that the daughter of the Duke of Windermere, having a little Royal blood in her veins, could become the wife of Prince Paul.

"We were so lucky, so very, very lucky!" Princess Louise had said over and over again to Zorina. "I loved your father from the moment I saw him, and he fell in love with me. If I had not been allowed to marry him, I would have wanted to die!"

She had been thinking of herself and not her daughter as she spoke.

She did not realise that in Zorina's mind it was deeply engraved that she must fall in love as her mother and father had done.

Any other kind of marriage, she thought, would be not only frightening but intolerable.

It was something, however, that she felt too shy to say to her mother or anyone else.

As they walked along the corridor escorted by a Lady-in-Waiting and one of the Queen's *Aides-de-Camp* to where Her Majesty was waiting, she told herself she was certain the Queen was not concerned with her marriage.

There must, therefore, be some other reason for her having sent for them so hurriedly and unexpectedly.

There was a great fussing and whispering outside the Queen's Room, then the *Aide-de-Camp* went in and a few minutes later returned to say:

"Her Majesty will receive Your Royal Highness."

Princess Louise walked ahead, with Zorina following her, and her first impression of the room was that she had never seen so many pictures and photographs.

They were everywhere, on every piece of furniture, and on the rich crimson flock of the walls.

Zorina was to learn later that there were nearly two hundred and fifty of them and they were carried from

Windsor to Balmoral and Osborne every time the Queen moved.

Her servants often found her looking round at them as she played patience in the evenings by the light of two wax candles in the big chandeliers.

In the daytime she picked over her other treasures with her fat heavily-beringed fingers.

There were bundles of letters, paper-weights, inkstands, dead flowers, old penknives, and sheets of music.

Zorina could see Her Majesty's Birthday Book, lying prominently on a table, full of the signatures of her visitors.

The Queen took it with her wherever she went and the Princess had said laughingly it was sometimes mistaken for a Bible.

Zorina was aware of a small figure in black wearing a white cap seated at the far end of the room.

Because the Queen was always spoken of in such awe, and she had not seen her since she was twelve, she had imagined her to be a rather large, overpowering woman.

Instead, she looked small and somehow older than she had expected.

She held out her hand as Princess Louise made a deep curtsy, then having kissed the Queen's hand, she kissed her cheek.

"It is nice to see you, Louise! How are you?"

"Very well, thank you, Ma'am."

The Queen's eyes moved towards Zorina.

Zorina obediently curtsied as her mother had done, and kissed the Queen's hand.

Then, as she rose, the Queen said:

"You may sit down."

Princess Louise took the chair nearest to her and Zorina sat a little farther away.

Then they waited in what Zorina thought was a deliberately planned awe-inspiring silence.

"I have asked you here," the Queen began at last, "to tell you that I have decided to give my approval to Victoria Mary marrying King Otto of Leothia!"

Princess Louise gave a little gasp, and Zorina felt as if she had been turned to stone.

"That is . . . very gracious of you, Ma'am," Princess Louise managed to stammer with some difficulty.

"I thought, Louise, that you would be pleased," the Queen said. "After all, with so much unrest in so many countries, it is difficult to find a reigning King who is not already married."

"I thought . . ." Princess Louise began hesitatingly.

". . . that he was married," the Queen finished. "That was true until two years ago, when his wife, a pleasant woman, died."

The Queen fixed her eyes on Zorina as she went on:

"His Majesty is now asking for an English wife, as he feels, quite rightly, that to be associated with our nation will strengthen his position in Europe at a time when it is very necessary."

"I am afraid, Ma'am," Princess Louise admitted, "that I am not quite certain where Leothia is."

"I am sure your husband would have had no difficulty in locating it," the Queen said scathingly. "Leothia is a small but politically important country bordering on Austria to the North, Serbia to the West, Rumania to the East, and it just touches Bulgaria to the South."

"Yes . . . of course . . . I remember it now," Princess Louise said hastily.

"Its importance to us in England lies in the fact that it serves as a 'buffer' between the countries I have just mentioned, and will prevent them, or so I can only hope, from attacking each other."

"You . . . do not think . . . Ma'am," Princess Louise said tentatively, "that Victoria is a little . . . young for King Otto . . . who I now recall has a . . . grown-up family."

"I do not consider that age has anything to do with it!" the Queen replied sharply. "Victoria Mary comes from a respectable English family which has Royal connections, and your late-lamented husband had a lineage which we are well aware goes back into antiquity."

"Of which he was very proud, Ma'am!"

"And quite rightly," the Queen said, "but now that Parnassos has lost its Monarchy, you must realise it is unfortunately of little consequence in preserving the Balance of Power in Europe."

"Yes, Ma'am," the Princess replied meekly.

"In response to His Majesty King Otto's request," the Queen continued, "I looked around at what English Princesses were available, and there is nobody at the moment except for Victoria Mary. I am sure, Louise, you could not wish for a better marriage for your only child."

"No, of course not, Ma'am."

"You are aware she will become a reigning Queen over a very attractive country?"

"I do understand that, Ma'am," Princess Louise said, "and I am very grateful."

"And you, Victoria Mary," the Queen said sharply. "I hope you, too, are grateful?"

"I was just wondering, Ma'am," Zorina replied, "how old King Otto is. Mama said he had a grown-up family."

The Queen glared at her as if she thought the question impertinent before she answered somewhat grudgingly:

"I suppose His Majesty must be nearing sixty, but his age is unimportant. He is a King, Victoria, and you will be his Queen. That should be sufficient for any young girl!"

Zorina did not speak, and the Queen said in an even more sharp tone, as if she felt thwarted:

"I feel it would be a mistake for there to be another Queen Victoria in Europe at the moment, and I believe you have another name."

"Yes, Ma'am," Princess Louise replied. "Zorina is what my daughter is always called by the family."

The Queen raised her eye-brows as if she thought it slightly flamboyant, perhaps theatrical. Then she said:

"It is, I suppose, suitable for Leothia. So, Victoria, in future you will be known by your third name, and at least it will be original amongst the thrones of Europe."

"Thank . . . you, Ma'am."

Zorina did not sound very grateful, and Princess Louise said gushingly:

"I cannot begin to thank you, Ma'am, for all your kindness. It will be wonderful for Zorina at such an early age to be a Queen, and also I know it will make her happy to keep her own name, which was specially chosen for her by her father."

"Then that is settled!" the Queen said. "And now..."

Before she could go any further, Zorina said:

"Please...Ma'am, when am I to...meet...the King?"

She was thinking frantically that if she disliked him, she might find some means of escaping from the marriage.

"His Majesty, not unnaturally," the Queen answered, "finds it impossible to make the journey to England himself. He has sent his son as his representative, whom you will meet tonight at dinner."

"I would have liked to meet His Majesty himself," Zorina persisted, "before the arrangements for the wedding are made."

"That is completely out of the question!" the Queen said in an exasperated tone. "I have already arranged that you and your mother will leave for Leothia in three weeks' time."

Zorina gave a gasp of horror.

"In...three...weeks, Ma'am?"

As if the Princess realised from the sound of her daughter's voice that she was about to be difficult, she intervened:

"I am sure, Ma'am, that Zorina is thinking of her trousseau. Three weeks will not give us time to make any gowns, and we do not have the money to buy anything that is expensive."

The Princess spoke humbly.

At the same time, she was very much aware that Zorina was vibrating almost violently against the haste in which everything was being done.

"I had already intended, if you had given me a

chance to speak of it," the Queen replied, "to give Zorina her trousseau as a wedding present."

"That is very kind of you, Ma'am."

"It is what I have done, as you should be aware, Louise, for a number of other brides, and I think it more appropriate in your case than a piece of jewellery when there will doubtless be a large collection of jewels waiting for Zorina in Leothia."

"I can only say thank you, thank you very, very much, Ma'am!" the Princess said.

"As to all this nonsense from Zorina about meeting the King before all the arrangements are made," Queen Victoria went on, "such a thing is completely and absolutely impossible."

She gave Zorina a scathing look before she continued:

"What you should do is to go down on your knees and be grateful that you have been chosen not only for such a responsible position, but also to be an Ambassador for your country."

She paused before she went on:

"You will see to it that the British are respected and admired in Leothia, as they are in other countries to which we have given our support, and where I have provided members of my own family to be the Consorts of reigning Monarchs."

The note of satisfaction in the Queen's voice was very noticeable.

Then she added:

"I will have, Zorina, a private talk with you before you leave to make quite sure you are aware of what is expected of you as Queen of Leothia."

"Now I must rest before I receive the Prime Minister who, I understand, is waiting to see me."

"Yes, of course, Ma'am," Princess Louise replied, rising to her feet. "And thank you again from the bottom of my heart for your kindness and consideration."

She curtsied as she spoke and again kissed the Queen's hand and her cheek, and Zorina followed her.

Only as she touched the Queen's hand with her lips did the Queen say:

"You are a pretty child, but it is more important to have brains, and I shall expect you to use your intelligence when you reach Leothia. Do you understand?"

"Yes . . . Ma'am."

Zorina backed away from the Queen as her mother was doing.

As they left the room she was aware that the Lady-in-Waiting and the *Aide-de-Camp* who were standing outside looked at her with curiosity.

She was sure they were aware of what had taken place and that now that she was to be a Queen, they were regarding her in a new and very different light.

It was not until much later that she was able to tell her mother what she was thinking.

The Lady-in-Waiting who went with them down the passage took them to a Sitting-Room, where tea was waiting.

There they were joined by another Lady-in-Waiting and an elderly man who Zorina learned was the Master of the Queen's Household.

They talked to Princess Louise, ignoring Zorina, as she expected.

Yet, at the same time, she was aware there were calculating glances in her direction and she was being more or less "sized-up" by the two Ladies-in-Waiting.

Only when Princess Louise said she would like to rest before dinner and she thought Zorina would feel the same did they go to their bed-rooms.

As Zorina went into her mother's room she said:

"It is ridiculous, Mama! How can I possibly marry a man who is nearly sixty? He is older than Papa would now be!"

The Princess looked round to be quite certain that the door was closed before she said:

"I know it seems rather frightening, Dearest, but think what it will mean to you."

"That is what I *am* thinking!" Zorina said. "Which is why you have to tell the Queen that I will not do it!"

"Zorina! Zorina!" the Princess pleaded. "How can you be so foolish and so stupid! You will be a Queen! Think what it will mean to be respected, admired, and to be able to live in the luxury we have been unable to have ever since Papa died."

"B-but . . . Mama . . . he will be my . . . husband!"

Zorina could not say any more.

She was thinking that old though the King was, he would want to kiss her and perhaps touch her.

The idea made her shudder.

She wanted to be married, of course she did, but to a young man, somebody like Rudolf.

She saw his handsome face in front of her eyes, and she could hear his deep voice telling her how beautiful she was.

That was what she wanted to hear.

She wanted to know that the man she married excited her as she had been this morning when she knew she would see Rudolf again.

"I cannot do it, Mama!"

Princess Louise gave a cry of horror.

"But you must, Zorina, you must! Can you not understand? If you refuse to do as the Queen commands, she may ostracise us and even turn us out of our apartment at Hampton Court Palace! Then we will have nowhere to go!"

"You cannot mean that, Mama!"

"She could turn us out in the street to-morrow," Princess Louise said. "We would then have to go crawling to my brother, your Uncle Lionel, who told me in a letter last week that he is having to sell land because he is so hard-up."

Zorina did not reply.

She only sat down on the edge of her mother's bed, feeling suddenly very weak, as if she could not stand up any longer.

She knew as she did so that she was facing the inevitable, and there was nothing she could do about it.

The Queen had given her orders, and whatever she felt about them, she had to obey.

chapter three

DRESSING for dinner, Zorina was still wondering if there was any way by which she could tell Rudolf why she was unable to meet him to-morrow morning.

She imagined him arriving early, looking out of the window as he was doing the first time she had bumped into him.

He would be finding it difficult to understand that she was not coming.

"Why did I not find out where he was staying?" she asked herself a thousand times.

There was no answer, and she tried, instead, to be as excited as her mother wanted her to be at wearing her new gown.

Princess Louise had made it very skilfully and it was exceedingly attractive.

The bodice fitted tightly and revealed the tininess of

her waist. Chiffon trimmed the *décolletage* and cascaded behind her into a small draped bustle.

It would have been wrong for anyone so young to have an exaggerated bustle, as was worn by the more flamboyant Beauties in London.

Princess Louise thought privately that when her daughter was finally dressed, she looked exquisitely beautiful.

"It is a lovely gown, Mama, and you have made it very, very cleverly!" Zorina exclaimed.

Nevertheless, she could not resist wishing that Rudolf could see her in it.

Because she was frightened when she thought of the future and the King whom she must marry, she tried to put him out of her thoughts and enjoy being at the Castle.

She was attending the first important Dinner-party at which she had ever been a guest.

Twice since they had returned to England, Princess Louise had taken Zorina to stay with her brother, the Duke of Windermere.

To be honest, after the beauty of Hampton Court, Zorina had been disappointed.

The house which belonged to her uncle was large but not particularly attractive.

Because the Duke was permanently hard-up, Zorina was aware that the pictures, of which there were a considerable number, needed cleaning, many of the carpets were threadbare, and the curtains faded.

There were also not enough servants for such a large establishment.

The Duke and Duchess were continually complaining

of the expenses which inevitably mounted up on the estate.

It prevented them from entertaining as much as they would have liked, neither could they afford to open Windermere House in London.

The Princess had been delighted to see her brother again and to meet her nephews and nieces, but she realised that the girls, who were as yet unmarried, looked at Zorina enviously.

The boys were interested only in horses and dogs rather than in talking to what they described amongst themselves as "that foreign girl."

The visits, therefore, had not been a great success.

When in the last two years there had been no invitation to Windermere, neither Zorina nor her mother had been particularly disappointed.

It was exciting, however, to be in Windsor Castle.

What was more, because the Dinner-party was, as the Princess told her, being given for her, she had an importance she had never had before.

At the same time, as her mother instructed her over and over again on how she should behave, Zorina could not help thinking that it would be far more fun to be wandering through Hampton Court Palace with Rudolf.

"Perhaps he will be there the day after to-morrow," she told herself consolingly.

He might, however, have already left, and she would not be able even to say good-bye to him.

When the Princess was ready, they walked through the labyrinth of passages which were noted as being so complicated that guests were often lost.

Once, Zorina was told, a visitor got lost on his way

51

to bed, and was forced to spend the night on a sofa in the State Gallery.

When a house-maid found him in the morning, she supposed him to be drunk, and fetched a Policeman.

Zorina thought this was funny, but she was even more amused when she was told that one Gentleman spent nearly an hour wandering about the corridors trying to identify his bed-room.

"At length," the Lady-in-Waiting related, "he opened a door and found to his horror the Queen having her hair brushed by a maid."

"That must have been very embarrassing!" Zorina exclaimed.

"It was," the Lady-in-Waiting agreed, "and something everybody new here is frightened will happen to them."

The Princess, however, found their way to the White Drawing-Room, where they were to meet before dinner.

It was a pretty room with a huge chandelier suspended from an ornate ceiling and portraits of the Royal Family set in elaborate gilt panels.

Zorina thought the heavily carved gilt furniture was very appropriate for Kings and Queens.

There were a number of people standing about when they entered, and the Lord Chamberlain, having greeted them, began to introduce each guest to Princess Louise.

They all seemed to Zorina to be rather old.

But the ladies glittering with diamonds were no more spectacular than the men in knee-breeches and their cutaway coats clustered with decorations.

A number of them were also wearing the blue ribbon of the Order of the Garter.

As they shook hands one after another with Princess

Louise, then herself, she heard the Lord Chamberlain say:

"Now, Your Royal Highness, I want you to meet our guest of honour who is the representative of King Otto of Leothia—Prince Rudolf!"

Because the name was familiar, Zorina looked quickly to see who was standing beside the Lord Chamberlain.

As she did so, she felt her heart turn over in her breast.

It was Rudolf who stood there, Rudolf, looking quite different from when she had seen him this morning.

Now he was wearing the white jacket of a military uniform with gold epaulettes and a number of decorations.

But it was Rudolf—there was no mistaking him!

Then, as the Lord Chamberlain introduced them, their eyes met and she knew that he was as astonished as she was.

As she touched his hand and for a moment forgot to curtsy, everything seemed to fade away, the Drawing-Room, the people standing around them, the Lord Chamberlain, and her mother.

Instead, there was only Rudolf, and as she looked at him she saw the expression in his eyes change.

What they said to each other she could never afterwards remember, but it must have seemed quite acceptable to the Princess.

A minute later the Queen came into the room and everybody instinctively lined up to be presented or to curtsy as she passed them.

"It cannot be true!" Zorina was saying to herself as the Queen proceeded into dinner on the arm of Prince

Rudolf, while she was escorted by the Lord Chamberlain.

"I must be dreaming!" she murmured as she sat down at the table with Rudolf on the Queen's right and herself on his other side.

She had been warned by her mother that dinner in the Royal Presence was a trial because the Queen's guests were expected to speak quietly, in fact little above a whisper.

"If ever Her Majesty overhears what she believes to be an excessive exhilaration in the conversation," the Princess had said, "or laughter and lack of delicacy at the other end of the table, she will indicate her disapproval."

"How frightening, Mama!" Zorina exclaimed.

"It is," Princess Louise agreed, "and after that the meal continues in an embarrassing silence."

The Queen now was having what sounded like a very banal conversation with Rudolf.

Zorina realised that the others at the table were talking in little more than a whisper.

It was impossible for Zorina not to listen to what the Queen was saying to Rudolf rather than talk to the gentleman on her other side.

He was, she thought, very old, and rather deaf.

She noted that the Queen wore on her wrist a large diamond bracelet, in the centre of which was a miniature of the Prince Consort and a lock of his hair.

It made her remember that Her Majesty had married the man she loved.

She wondered whether, if the next day she told the Queen that she could not marry the King of Leothia because he was so old, she would understand.

Then she remembered what the Queen had already said about age being unimportant, and knew that Her Majesty would not understand, and would be extremely angry.

With an effort she tried to pay attention to what was happening around her rather than think of herself.

The gold plate, the beautiful Sèvres china, the two Indian servants behind the Queen's chair, made it all seem somehow unreal.

There was a Highlander to pour out the wine, and Zorina found that dinner was served quickly, the moment she finished one dish, another being put in front of her.

But the meal was long and elaborate.

There was course after course—three or four choices of meat, a hot pudding and an iced one, a savoury, and all kinds of hot-house fruit.

Zorina found it difficult to realise what she was eating as she was waiting breathlessly for the moment she could speak to Rudolf.

However, because the Queen liked young men, especially when they were handsome, it was a long time before she turned to the gentleman on her other side.

"This cannot be true!"

Rudolf was speaking in his deep voice in a very low tone.

"That . . . is what I . . . thought when I saw . . . you."

"Why did you not tell me?"

"There never . . . seemed to be . . . time."

There was silence. Then Rudolf said:

"How could I have known—how could I have guessed who you were?"

There was a note of pain in his voice.

When Zorina looked into his eyes, she knew what she had seen in them just after they had been introduced.

"I was . . . worrying," she said, "because . . . I would not be . . . able to meet you . . . to-morrow morning."

"I had already decided," he answered, "that I would leave here very early and reach Hampton Court so that I could wait for you."

Before she could reply, Rudolf's glass was refilled, and when the servant moved away, he said:

"Did you know this morning that you were coming here?"

"No . . . of course . . . not," Zorina replied. "My Nurse was waiting for me when I . . . reached the Prince's apartment . . . to tell me that a . . . messenger had just . . . arrived from . . . the Castle."

"And I, too, found a message waiting for me when I returned."

"You . . . you did not . . . tell me where that . . . was."

"I have been staying with a relative of mine who married a British Ambassador and moved to Hampton Court before I was born. She is very old, and it was what you might call 'a duty visit.' "

"And you did not . . . mind when you were . . . told to come to . . . Windsor Castle . . . sooner than you . . . expected?"

"I minded because I was leaving you."

The way he spoke made Zorina give a little quiver, and as if he were aware of it, he said:

"I have to talk to you alone!"

"You know . . . that is not . . . possible."

"It has to be!"

"But . . . how? What . . . can we . . . do?"

As Zorina spoke, she looked nervously over Rudolf's shoulder and saw with relief that the Queen was still talking to the Gentleman on her other side.

At the same time, she was aware that all down the table there were eyes watching her and Rudolf.

She was quite certain her fellow guests would be speculating as to what they were saying to each other.

As if he were aware of what she was thinking, he said after a moment:

"I will find some way so that we can meet. Leave it to me!"

Zorina wanted to say she was very happy to leave everything to him.

Then, as she helped herself automatically to the next course, she remembered that Rudolf was here to represent her father, the King, whom she was to marry!

It all seemed unreal, a fantasy, like the long table in front of her, the glitter of jewels, the pomposity of the Gentlemen loaded with their decorations.

'It is all a dream,' she thought. 'I shall wake up and find that nothing is happening to me except that I can walk through the deserted State-Rooms of the Palace on my way to my lessons.'

It was a quarter-to-eleven before the dinner came to an end and the Queen rose from the table.

She went out of the Dining-Room and into another room, where they were served with coffee and liqueurs.

There was a chair, and in front of it a little table where the Queen seated herself.

The guests stood in a circle a considerable distance from her and the Queen sipped her coffee while a page held the saucer on a gold salver.

The guests talked amongst themselves, but still in the

low voices they had used in the Dining-Room.

The Queen beckoned Princess Louise, and after she had talked to her, obviously, Zorina thought, about Leothia, Rudolf was summoned to her side.

With him the Queen became quite animated, smiling and even laughing.

Then they all moved into the White Drawing-Room, where they stood while the Queen talked first to one person, then to another.

Finally, Rudolf came to Zorina's side and it seemed quite natural for them to move a little way behind the other guests.

"Listen," he said in a voice that only she could hear, "I remember that there is a Sitting-Room almost opposite the bed-room in which you are sleeping."

Zorina looked at him in surprise, and he explained:

"I was here three years ago with my mother, and I have been able to ascertain that you are in the same room that she used."

Zorina made a little murmur to show she understood, and he went on:

"When you retire to bed, wait until you think everybody is safely in their bed-rooms, then join me in the Sitting-Room."

Zorina, with a little tremor of fear, looked to where her mother was standing.

She knew how angry she would be if she realised what was being planned in Windsor Castle, of all places!

"I *have* to talk to you!" Rudolf insisted. "And now that the Queen has expedited matters, I may have to leave to-morrow."

"For . . . where?"

"I have to be in London for one night, then go North on some business that my father entrusted to me as I was coming to England."

Zorina looked at him, feeling it hard to understand what he was saying.

She was only acutely conscious of how handsome he looked and how different from the young man to whom she had talked so easily for the last two mornings.

"You will come?" he asked.

"Y-yes . . . I will try."

He had to be content with that.

Knowing that if they were together much longer people would talk about it, he turned in what seemed a perfectly natural way to the lady nearest to them, saying:

"I was just telling Princess Zorina, Duchess, how beautiful my country is! You have visited Leothia, so I know you will agree that I am not exaggerating its loveliness."

"No, of course you are not, Your Royal Highness," the Duchess replied, "and I know the Princess, if she ever goes there, will find it fascinating."

Almost as if the Duchess had given a cue to the Queen, who was on the other side of the room, Zorina heard the Lord Chamberlain say:

"Her Majesty wishes to speak!"

There was an instant silence, and the Queen, looking towards Zorina, said:

"I think some of you know already that the Dinner-party to-night which was given in honour of His Royal Highness Prince Rudolf of Leothia was a notable occasion because he is representing his father. His Majesty

King Otto has received my permission to marry into my family!"

Zorina thought that one or two people gave a little gasp before the Queen went on:

"It is with great pleasure that I have given my seal of approval to the marriage of His Majesty King Otto and Her Royal Highness Princess Zorina—as she will be known in future—of Parnassos."

Now there was undoubtedly a murmur of surprise and excitement, and the Queen said sharply, as if she felt she had been interrupted:

"Come here, Zorina!"

Feeling shy, Zorina walked to the Queen's chair and sank down in a deep curtsy.

"Now," the Queen said, "you are officially engaged, and I have already arranged for it to be announced tomorrow in the Court Circular."

The way she spoke told Zorina that she was trapped and there was no escape.

She had the feeling, although, of course, it was absurd, that the Queen was aware of her rebellious feelings and was making sure that it would be impossible for her to express them.

It was then the Lord Chamberlain took over, saying:

"As we all have a glass in our hands, I propose that we drink to the future happiness of Her Royal Highness Princess Zorina, and send His Majesty King Otto our warmest congratulations on attaining a very charming and beautiful English bride!"

There was a murmur of approval, and glasses were raised.

Zorina, who was now standing beside the Queen, found it impossible not to look at Rudolf, and saw that while he held his glass in the correct manner, he did not drink from it.

She knew without words that he was feeling as she was, that they were both caught in a vortex from which there was no escape.

*   *   *

Zorina opened her bed-room door very, very softly.

She was frightened, very frightened.

Yet she knew that if there had been soldiers barring the way with drawn swords, she would still have gone to meet Rudolf.

Because Nanny was waiting up for her mother and for herself to undo their gowns and see them into bed, there was no question of her remaining dressed.

She had, therefore, covered her nightdress with the same blue woollen dressing-gown she had worn for the last five years.

It was a little short and rather tight, but its colour combined with the candle she carried in her hand seemed to pick out the red in her hair.

It made her eyes look even larger than they were ordinarily.

Then, as she peeped out into the corridor, she saw that it was not dark as she had expected.

There were a few candles still alight in the silver sconces so that there was no need to take her own.

She set it down on a table just inside the door and went back to look first one way, then the other, to make quite sure there was no one about.

When she and the Princess came up to bed, she had looked for the Sitting-Room of which Rudolf had spoken.

She had seen because the door was half-open that it was, in fact, only a few yards from her bed-room.

There had been only one candle burning in it, she thought, but now, when she opened the door, the room seemed quite brightly lit.

Rudolf was standing in front of the fireplace still wearing his decorations.

Moving swiftly inside, Zorina shut the door behind her, then stood looking at him.

For some seconds neither of them moved. Then he said:

"You have come! How could you be so brave, so wonderful?"

"I . . . I am . . . frightened!" Zorina said in a very small voice.

It was then he walked towards her, while she did not move.

She had the strangest feeling that he was about to put his arms around her, but instead he turned and locked the door.

Then, taking her hand, he drew her towards the sofa, and she felt herself tremble because he was touching her.

As they sat down he said:

"My darling, how could this have happened to us?"

She stared at him in surprise and he said roughly:

"What is the use of pretending? I fell in love with you the moment I saw you, and all to-day I have been thinking of nothing but how quickly I could get back to the Palace to tell you so."

"B-but you . . . must not . . . say such things!" Zorina stammered.

At the same time, she felt as if a light had been lit

within her, and her whole body had come alive.

Rudolf loved her!

As she looked into his handsome face so near to hers, she knew that what she had been feeling about him also was love, although she had not realised it.

"I knew to-day," he went on, "when I left Hampton Court to come here, that the only thing that mattered to me was that I should get back as quickly as possible to see you, and to tell you of my love."

Zorina made a little sound that was almost like a cry of an animal in pain, and he said:

"You realise there is nothing we can do?"

"Nothing!"

"If I were behaving properly," Rudolf went on as if he were working it out for himself, "I should not tell you of my feelings, and I suppose you might never have guessed what I feel."

"I . . . knew what . . . I felt," Zorina whispered.

She looked into his eyes as she spoke and thought he would now put his arms around her.

If he kissed her, it would be the most wonderful thing that could ever happen.

Instead, he rose to his feet.

"I am behaving abominably, inexcusably," he said, "and you have to forgive me."

"There is . . . nothing to . . . forgive," Zorina whispered.

"All I know is that I love you! And I am asking Fate, or the gods, why this should happen to me!"

Zorina drew in her breath.

The agony in his voice was, she knew, an inexpressible pain that she had never heard before in her whole life.

"The . . . the Queen told me . . . to-day that I had to . . . m-marry . . . King Otto," she said in a hesitating little voice, "but I . . . told Mama that I could not . . . do so."

"And what did your mother say?"

"She said I . . . had to . . . otherwise the Queen would be very . . . angry . . . and she might . . . even turn us . . . out of our Grace and Favour apartment . . . and we would have . . . nowhere to go!"

"It is intolerable," Rudolf exclaimed, "absolutely intolerable that you should be in such a position!"

"But . . . we are, and Mama has been so . . . unhappy since Papa was . . . killed. We have been so . . . very poor . . . so you can understand she is glad that I should . . . marry anyone so . . . important."

"And you? What do you think?"

His voice was hard, and she thought if he had not been keeping his voice low, he would have shouted at her.

"I . . . I am . . . frightened, and also . . . I know now that I . . . love you!"

As she spoke, the tears ran down her cheeks.

Rudolf crossed the room to kneel beside her.

"My precious, my darling, do not cry!" he begged. "I cannot bear you to be unhappy, and I would rather kill myself than hurt you."

"Why did this . . . have to . . . happen to . . . us?" Zorina asked as he had.

He looked down at her hand which he had taken in his.

"If I have to be crucified," he said after a moment, "I would rather it was over you than anyone else!"

"H-how can I . . . marry your father . . . when I . . . love you?"

She saw before he spoke that it was a question she should not have asked him, knowing how much it would hurt him.

Gently he put her hand into her lap and rose to his feet.

He walked away from her, back to where he had been standing before, with his back to the empty mantelpiece.

"I have always known," he said, "that there were penalties for being Royal, but because I am the younger son I thought I might escape being pushed into marriage, because it was expedient, with some Princess who had no wish to marry me any more than I wished to marry her."

Zorina was listening, but there were tears in her eyes, although she had wiped away those that had run down her cheeks.

"Then when I saw you," Rudolf went on, "I thanked my lucky stars that I was of no political importance. I thought it might be difficult to get permission to marry you because I would have to have my father's consent, but I knew that I would fight to do so with every weapon in my power."

He paused before he said very movingly:

"If I were still refused permission, I had already made up my mind that I would denounce my rank and leave Leothia to live somewhere else in the world. That, Zorina, is how much I love you."

Again he hesitated before he asked:

"Would you have come with me?"

Zorina did not hesitate.

"You . . . know I would have . . . done so," she answered, "and it is . . . what I would . . . like to do . . . now."

"Do not say that," Rudolf cried, "for God's sake, do not say that!"

He looked away from her as he said:

"It is what I want to ask you to do, it is what every nerve and instinct in my body tells me I should do— with the exception of one fact which I cannot ignore."

"What is . . . that?" Zorina asked in a whisper.

"It is that I love my country, and I know how important you are to Leothia at this moment."

"Because . . . I am . . . English?" Zorina asked in a trembling voice.

"Because you have been chosen by the Queen of England, because with you comes strength and power and the Union Jack, to support and sustain our Monarchy."

Zorina gave a little cry and put up her hands.

"B-but . . . why me?" she asked. "Why could not . . . Mama have married your father? She is English . . . even more English than I am."

She thought, as she spoke, that Rudolf would not answer her. Then, as if he forced himself to do so, he said:

"My father would prefer a young Queen in order to increase his family, which consists only of two sons. He wants not only to make the succession sure, but also to make the Royal Family of Leothia known in other Courts in Europe."

For a moment Zorina did not take in what he was saying.

Then she realised, as if for the first time, that if she

were married to the King, old though he was, he would give her children.

She was very innocent and had no idea what happened between a man and a woman when they were married.

She knew it must be something very intimate and personal.

Although she had already felt horrified at the idea of the King kissing her, this was something far more terrifying.

It was something from which she shrank so that the fear of it seemed to run through her body like forked lightning.

Suddenly she sprang to her feet.

"I . . . I cannot . . . do it . . . I cannot marry him!" she cried. "H-how can you . . . expect me to do . . . anything so . . . horrible . . . when I . . . I love you?"

"We should not be talking like this," Rudolf said, "but I suppose it would have happened sooner or later."

Zorina did not reply.

She only stood looking at him, and he went on:

"There is nothing either of us can do but accept our fate from which there is no escape."

"B-but . . . I cannot . . . I cannot . . . do it!" Zorina said.

"You have to!" Rudolf answered. "It is the penalty we pay for being born who we are."

He looked at her, then away again before he said:

"I will take you to my father, but it will be impossible for me to stay to see you married, and I shall leave the country as soon as it has happened."

"Where . . . will you . . . go?"

"Does it matter? Around the world—to the top of the

Himalayas—to Africa! Anywhere so long as I am not tempted by being near you, by seeing your beauty, by hearing your voice."

His own voice broke on the last words.

He walked towards the window to draw aside the curtain, as if he felt he must have air in which to breathe.

After a moment he said, and his voice was harsh:

"Go to bed, Zorina, and try to forget me. I am behaving with a superhuman self-control which you are too young to understand."

"I . . . cannot leave you . . . like this, when we are both so . . . unhappy."

"If you stay, you will try me too far," Rudolf said. "I am trying to behave, as the English say, 'as a Gentleman,' but I am not an Englishman, Zorina."

He paused as if he were feeling for words before he said:

"In my country we are capable of great passion, and we burn like the heat of the sun."

Zorina listened, bewildered, but at the same time deeply moved by the agony in his voice which told her he was suffering unbearably.

"I want you!" Rudolf was saying. "I want to hold you in my arms and kiss you until you cry for mercy. I want to light a fire within you from the blazing furnace which consumes me, utterly and completely!"

He made a sound that was almost a sob before he said:

"This morning, when we were close to each other, I would have sworn before God Himself that we were made for each other, and nothing could divide us."

His voice rose a little and became somewhat louder as he said:

"It is too late! Do you hear, Zorina? It is too late, and now — for God's sake — go, and leave me alone!"

Zorina was already trembling. His last words were spoken with a desperation which she felt came from the very depths of his heart.

It made her understand that she must drive him no further.

With tears running down her cheeks, she stood looking at the back of his dark head, his hand that was clutching the curtain desperately, as if for support.

Then she turned, and moving soundlessly across the room in her slippers she reached the door.

As she turned the key in the lock she looked back and said very softly:

"I . . . I love you with . . . all my heart . . . and I will never . . . love anyone else!"

Then she ran across the passage and back into her room.

She threw herself down on the bed to cry tempestuously and hopelessly, until she was utterly exhausted.

chapter four

THERE was no sign of Rudolf when Zorina left Windsor Castle the next morning with her mother.

The Princess was excited over the thought of Zorina's trousseau.

She had already arranged through one of the Ladies-in-Waiting that the best dressmakers which were patronised by the Queen should come to Hampton Court Palace for their orders.

"We must also go to Bond Street," the Princess said, "and at last, Dearest, I will see you elegantly dressed as I have always longed for you to be."

Zorina wished she could feel more enthusiastic about it.

But all she could think of was the pain in Rudolf's voice before she had left him last night, and of the hopelessness of her future.

She was sure he was speaking the truth when he said that he would not remain in Leothia after she was married.

Now she thought how terrifying it would be to live in a strange country where there was no one she loved.

For the first time she realised that everything that was planned was laid out in front of her like a map.

The glamour had gone and it was, in fact, horrifying.

"I thought Prince Rudolf was a charming young man," the Princess was saying, "and I am sure he will look after us on the journey out, and tell you what to expect when you arrive."

Zorina did not speak, and the Princess continued:

"The Lord Chamberlain told me we are to travel very grandly with a private coach attached to the Express, and it is something I shall look forward to myself."

She gave a little laugh as she said:

"I shall certainly need a new gown, for you must not be ashamed of your mother."

"I could never be that!" Zorina answered. "And, Mama, you are so beautiful that I cannot think why you cannot marry the King instead of me."

Zorina knew the answer, but she had spoken spontaneously, wanting to pay her mother a compliment.

Now, remembering what Rudolf had said about the King wanting more children, she felt herself shudder as if she were very cold.

"I met an old friend last night," Princess Louise said as if she were following her own thoughts. "He was quite a young Diplomat when your father and I knew him in Greece."

She paused for a moment before she continued:

"Now he tells me he has been appointed as the new British Ambassador to Leothia."

She smiled as she added:

"That means if I ask him to do so, I know he will look after you, Dearest, and you can consult him if you are in any difficulty."

Zorina thought the difficulties she would be in would not be something she could discuss with anyone except perhaps her mother.

There was no point, however, in saying so, and she only felt despairingly that she was being swept along on a tidal wave.

Almost before she was aware of what was happening, she would find herself in Leothia.

The next few days were so filled with activity over her trousseau that she hardly had time to think.

In fact, she fell asleep almost as soon as her head touched her pillow.

At the same time, every morning before the Princess came down for breakfast, she slipped away to the Cartoon Room.

It was just in case by some miraculous chance Rudolf was there waiting for her.

It was a forlorn hope, but still she waited, looking out of the windows with blind eyes.

All she could see was Rudolf's face, hear his voice, and feel their vibrations touching each other as they had moved side by side in the Palace.

"I love him! I love him, and it would be impossible for me ever to find another man so attractive!" Zorina whispered.

Then she could hear his voice saying:

"There is nothing either of us can do but accept our fate from which there is no escape."

Yet he loved her.

She would repeat to herself over and over again when he had said, his voice deep with passion:

"I want you! I want to hold you in my arms and kiss you until you cry for mercy. I want to light a fire within you from the blazing furnace which consumes me utterly and completely!"

That was the love she had always wanted: the love that was omnipotent and irresistible.

Instead, she had to marry an old man because he wanted more children.

"You are very pale, Dearest," the Princess said. "I know how tiring it is having so many fittings, and standing for so long. But think how lovely you will look when you reach Leothia."

'Lovely for whom?' Zorina wanted to ask, and knew the answer.

For the first time in her life she found that she was of importance.

The Prime Minister, who was also the Foreign Secretary, the Marquess of Salisbury, came to Hampton Court Palace to talk to her.

To her surprise he told her mother he would like to speak to her alone and she realised it was because he thought she might feel constrained if there was anybody else present.

"I believe Her Majesty the Queen has already explained to you the importance of Leothia as a buffer State between four other countries?" the Marquess began.

"Yes . . . My Lord."

"It would be a great help if you could impress that upon the King."

Zorina looked at him in surprise.

"But . . . surely His Majesty must be . . . aware of it . . . already?"

She had the idea that the Marquess was finding it a little difficult to answer her before he said:

"You have heard the saying 'it is difficult to see the wood for the trees'? In other words, Your Royal Highness, those who are on the outside and a little further away from the problems of those directly involved in them have a better view."

Zorina understood what he was trying to say and after a moment she asked:

"Do you really believe, if you are honest, My Lord, that the King will pay any attention to my ideas or opinions?"

She knew the Marquess was surprised, but he answered:

"I feel sure that anyone as beautiful as Your Royal Highness, and also so intelligent, will find it easy to make His Majesty, or anyone else, listen to what you have to say."

"I hope . . . you are . . . right," Zorina said in a small voice. "It is, however, rather . . . frightening that you expect so . . . much of me just because I am partly . . . English."

"Which means," the Marquess said firmly, "that you have the support of Her Majesty and my Cabinet behind you."

"Unfortunately you will all be a great distance away!" Zorina remarked.

"I am sure you will find our Ambassador, Lord Melbray, a great help," the Marquess replied. "Your mother has just been telling me that he is an old friend."

Zorina did not answer, and he went on as if he were thinking it out:

"It is a pity that Lord Melbray's wife is dead, because I am sure you would have found her a delightful person, as we all did. But there will, I am sure, be a number of English Ladies in Leothia and you can choose one of them to be your Lady-in-Waiting."

This was another aspect that Zorina had not considered, that as Queen she would have Ladies-in-Waiting to watch over her.

She felt as if this added even more bars to the cage in which she was about to be confined.

The Marquess, however, was very kind and told her that he had visited Leothia.

He described the beauty of the mountains and the charm of its people who had, of course, intermarried with the countries on either side of them.

"One thing I have already ascertained," Zorina told him, "is that I shall not find the language at all difficult. I can, of course, speak Austrian fluently, and I have a little knowledge of Rumanian."

She felt she was boasting but went on:

"Serbian is a little more difficult, but, of course, all the languages owe a lot to Greek, which makes it easier for me."

"I have already learned how talented you are," the Marquess replied, "and I am not exaggerating when I tell you that none of Her Majesty's relatives who have married recently have had as much intelligence as is attributed to you."

Zorina smiled at the compliment.

At the same time, she was well aware that the Marquess was doing everything in his power to make her look forward to being the Queen of Leothia.

She had the uncomfortable feeling, however, that there was a great deal he did not say.

It was only after he had left that she became aware that he had evaded very skilfully answering any direct questions about the King.

She felt perceptively that the Marquess had more or less admitted that King Otto was not behaving exactly as the British wished.

He had said nothing specifically to support this idea, and yet she was sure it was true.

She wondered whether on the journey she would dare to ask Rudolf to talk to her frankly about his father, and whether he would be brave enough to answer her questions.

In one aspect the three weeks before she left for Leothia seemed to Zorina to fly by because there was so much to do.

In another, they were intolerably slow because, although she knew it was wrong, she was counting the hours until she could see Rudolf again.

Finally the last of the boxes containing her trousseau, a great pile of them, were delivered to their small apartment.

Nanny, grumbling that she had "only one pair of hands," packed the gowns into Zorina's new trunks which were part of her trousseau.

Zorina had been clever enough to persuade her mother, who had been very difficult about it, to have two new gowns for which the Queen would pay the bill.

"It is quite easy, Mama," she said, "I shall order a

gown that I know will suit you and, as we are almost the same height, you can fit it when I am too busy or too indisposed to do so."

"I could not possibly do such a thing!" the Princess expostulated.

"Do not be so stupid, Mama! You know as well as I do that you cannot afford a new gown, and if you buy one which is smart enough for the wedding and a hat to match, it will mean you and Nanny going hungry for months."

She saw her mother was unconvinced and went on:

"It would not matter to the Queen if I am one dress short, and if you do not agree to do as I suggest, I shall go to Windsor Castle and ask her point-blank to dress you as befits the mother of a Royal bride!"

Princess Louise gave a cry of horror.

"How can you think of doing anything so terrible?"

"I promise you that is what I will do unless you agree to what I say," Zorina insisted.

Finally, because there really was no money, the Princess capitulated.

Zorina persuaded her to have not only an exquisitely smart dress for the wedding, but also an evening-gown.

"The one you made for me will fit beautifully into my trousseau, and I have only worn it once," Zorina said, "while your best gown is almost in rags and, if we are truthful, very out of date!"

There were arguments and protests, but Zorina got her way.

The Princess could therefore afford a few new feathers for the hat in which she was to travel.

Nanny sewed a new velvet collar onto her travelling-cape, so that it did not look so shabby.

"Now you look lovely, Mama!" Zorina approved. "And do not forget, your young man will be with us!"

For a moment the Princess did not know to whom she was referring. Then, when she realised it was the British Ambassador, she said quickly:

"You must not call him my 'young man'! It is true that he lived near my home when I was young, and we used to dance together at the Hunt Balls, but once I had met your father, I never thought of him again!"

"But I am sure he thought of you!" Zorina said incorrigibly.

Later, when they were travelling in a very comfortable Drawing-Room coach attached to the train they had boarded at Ostend, Zorina knew she had been right in thinking that Lord Melbray still admired her mother.

He certainly made every effort to amuse and interest her, and as the journey progressed, Zorina thought she had not seen her mother look so happy for a long time.

It was difficult, however, for her to smile and talk with the rest of the party.

This consisted of the Leothian Foreign Secretary and his wife, and two other ladies who had been appointed as temporary Ladies-in-Waiting until she could choose her own.

There were two *Aides-de-Camp* of the King, who were both middle-aged, and Rudolf.

She had not seen him again before they met at the Station in London, where there were a number of people to see them off from the Leothian Embassy and from the Foreign Office.

The Marquess of Salisbury had come in his capacity as Foreign Secretary rather than as Prime Minister.

Once again he said to Zorina:

"I am relying on Your Royal Highness, and Lord Melbray will, I am sure, be sending me glowing reports on your progress."

He smiled before he added:

"I am sure that the moment they see you the Leothians will take you to their hearts. I need not say again how important you are to the Balance of Power at this particular moment."

It was while she was talking to the Marquess on the platform, which had been covered with a red carpet, that she had seen Rudolf arriving.

At the sight of him her heart leapt so violently in her breast that she felt almost as if she might faint.

Then, as he walked towards them, she knew the only thing she wanted to do was to fling herself into his arms and tell him how much she loved him.

She knew as he approached nearer that he deliberately avoided meeting her eyes, although she was certain he was as conscious of her as she was of him.

Then, while she had no idea of what the Marquess was saying, and could not hear the chatter around them, Rudolf came towards her.

"You must forgive me, Your Royal Highness," he said in a cold, impersonal voice, "for not being here to receive you as I should have been. Unfortunately the carriage which was bringing me was involved in an accident with a curricle."

"You were not . . . hurt?" Zorina exclaimed in a frightened tone.

"Only angry that I should be late for Your Royal Highness!" Rudolf replied.

He did not look directly at her as he spoke.

She knew from the coldness of his voice that he was

deliberately trying to isolate himself from her.

It was almost, she thought, with a sense of relief that he turned to the Marquess.

"I must apologise to you also, My Lord."

"It is quite unnecessary, Your Royal Highness!" the Marquess replied. "Our streets are becoming so crowded, and there are so many bad drivers, that we have an increasing number of accidents taking place, which I find extremely regrettable."

"It is the same in our major streets," Rudolf remarked.

Zorina was not listening.

She was only wondering if he was aware of how violently her heart was throbbing, or how handsome he looked in his travelling-cape.

She thought she must have forgotten how good-looking he was, and how in comparison every other man seemed to pale into insignificance.

"I love you! I love you!" she wanted to say, but she knew that he was aware of it.

Although he was controlling himself, she could feel his heart reaching out towards hers, and they were as indivisibly joined as if she were in his arms.

The Station Master, resplendent in gold braid, told the Marquess respectfully that it was time for the passengers to board the train.

There were a great number of people to whom Zorina had to say good-bye.

Then she was bowed aboard into their private coach, and those who were travelling with her followed.

As soon as the train started, the stewards brought coffee and even breakfast for those who were hungry.

Zorina found herself seated in a comfortable armchair by a window, and her mother was next to her.

The seat opposite her, however, was unoccupied, and it was only after the train had started that she realised it was intended for Rudolf.

But he was deliberately talking to one of the *Aides-de-Camp* on the other side of the coach.

Finally, and, it seemed, reluctantly, because Lord Melbray wanted to talk to him, he came and sat down.

"We have a long journey in front of us," the Ambassador remarked. "I think we shall be comfortable."

Rudolf looked as if he might disagree, but Lord Melbray continued:

"The Sleeper which has been attached to the train which we will board at Ostend is, I am told, the most up-to-date in the whole of Europe."

"I shall look forward to seeing it," Rudolf replied. "I have always been interested in trains, ever since I was a small boy."

"I have always heard that Your Royal Highness's chief interest was climbing," Lord Melbray remarked.

"It is true that I have climbed most of the mountains in my country, and I am planning at the moment an expedition to the Himalayas."

Zorina, who was listening, drew in her breath.

So he had meant it when he had said he would go away once she was married, and she thought despairingly she might never see him again.

"Now, that is very interesting . . ." Lord Melbray was remarking, but Zorina could listen no further.

She felt as if Rudolf had deliberately stuck a dagger into her breast, but by putting half the world between them he would never kill her love.

"Stay with . . . me! Stay . . . with me!" she wanted to beg.

She felt her thoughts flying towards him and thought he must be aware of them.

She did not see him once they had embarked on the ship that was to carry them from Tilbury to Ostend.

There was a private cabin for herself and her mother and another for the rest of the Ladies in the party.

At Ostend their Drawing-Room coach with a Sleeper attached to it was at a platform which was sealed off from other travellers.

It was only with a great deal of shunting and letting off of steam that they were finally attached to the Express.

Rudolf appeared to be everywhere except with her.

Zorina felt miserably that they would never have a chance to speak to each other before they reached Leothia.

When it was time to retire, after a delicious dinner accompanied by some excellent wines, she realised there were three bed-rooms in their coach.

These were to be occupied by her mother, herself, and Rudolf, and everybody else was accommodated in a separate sleeping-car.

As they went to their individual compartments, the Princess said:

"If there is one thing I hate, Dearest, it is trying to sleep in a train. Some people say that the sound of the wheels lulls them to sleep, but they keep me awake and make me afraid we might crash!"

"I am sorry, Mama. It is important you should sleep, as we have such a long journey ahead of us."

"I shall sleep," the Princess replied, "because Nanny

insisted that I bring a little laudanum with me."

"Oh, Mama," Zorina protested, "I am sure it is bad for you!"

"Of course it is!" the Princess agreed. "At the same time, it is better than looking hollow-eyed and pale-faced to-morrow."

"You must not do that!" Zorina said. "You were looking lovely to-day, and I know Lord Melbray thought so too."

"Oh, Zorina, you do have ridiculous ideas! I doubt if he has even noticed me! We were talking of old times, when we were both very young."

Zorina did not answer.

She merely thought that her mother was over-doing her nonchalance about Lord Melbray's attentions.

It was only when she had undressed that she realised that, her mother having taken laudanum, there was a chance she might be able to speak to Rudolf.

She pretended to herself that she was looking for the magazine she had been reading during the journey as she crept from her compartment into the Drawing-Room.

When the stewards had left them to retire to their own quarters in another part of the train, they had extinguished the lights.

Zorina, going to the seat at which she had sat all day, pulled back the curtains from the window to find there was a full moon whose silver light flooded through the window.

It enabled her to see the empty seats and a number of papers scattered about.

She waited, not even daring to pray that Rudolf would know where she was.

Then suddenly she was aware that he was there!

As he came quietly towards her she looked up at him, feeling that nothing else mattered except that they were alone, and together.

He sat down beside her and she saw that he was dressed as he had been before everyone retired to bed.

For a moment she just sat looking at him, with her hair falling over her shoulders and over the expensive new satin *négligée* that was part of her trousseau.

She raised her face to his, and for a long moment they looked at each other in the moonlight, and there was no need for words.

Then at last in a whisper, Zorina said:

"I . . . I had to . . . talk to you!"

"There is nothing to say!" Rudolf replied. "But somehow I knew you would be here."

"Mama will . . . not wake, and I . . . felt you would . . . hear me . . . calling for you."

"My precious, that is something you must not do!"

"Why not?" Zorina asked. "We are not . . . hurting anybody at this moment . . . and it will be . . . something to . . . remember."

There was a little silence before Rudolf said:

"How can you be so exquisitely lovely and look as if you had just dropped from the sky?"

Zorina gave a little sigh.

"If only we could go back there, and that was the end of our journey."

"I have never suffered," he said, "such agonies as these past weeks since I left you behind at the Castle. I thought the best thing I could do was to vanish off the face of the earth, hoping perhaps we might meet again in some other life."

"When you talk...like that...you have...forgotten one...thing," Zorina murmured.

"What is that?"

"That I am...feeling the same...and the only thing for me which...makes it necessary to stay...alive is that you are...somewhere...near me."

"My darling!"

He made a movement as if to touch her, then stopped himself from doing so.

"If you talk to me like that," he said, "I will go mad! I love you until I can see nothing but your face, hear nothing but your voice!"

He drew in his breath before he went on:

"This is a mistake! Because I know it is not only making it worse for me but also for you, we must not do this again."

"B-but...I have to talk...to you!" Zorina pleaded.

Rudolf shook his head.

"You know as well as I do that love does not stand still; it either increases or dies. Our love will never die! It will only increase until it overwhelms us, and we will not be able to resist it!"

Zorina knew exactly what he was saying, and after a long silence she said in a voice he could hardly hear:

"M-must we...resist it?"

"I am older than you," Rudolf said harshly, "and therefore I have to do what is right and prevent you from doing what is wrong."

"But...I cannot...help loving you," Zorina said pathetically.

"Nor I you," Rudolf replied. "But we have to think of my country and the people in England who are relying on you to represent them."

"Now you are talking like the Marquess of Salisbury!" Zorina said in a dull voice.

Rudolf gave a little laugh that had no humour in it before he said:

"I am talking like this because I dare not say what I want to say."

He looked at her and his voice deepened.

"I love you! I adore you! I worship you! You are everything I have sought for and thought I would never find in a woman. Now, as I said the last time we were together, it is too late! Too late!"

"It may be . . . too late to . . . change what we . . . have to do," Zorina said hesitantly. "At the same time . . . I do not think that a love like ours is . . . wrong because love . . . comes from . . . God!"

Rudolf made a broken sound and, taking her hand, he raised it to his lips.

He kissed it passionately and she quivered at the intensity of his lips.

Then he turned it over and kissed her palm.

It gave her a strange sensation she had never known before, almost as if the moonlight had entered her body and little shafts of it were running through her.

Rudolf raised his head.

"As I have already told you, my darling," he said, "I want you wildly, uncontrollably, but instead I shall kneel at your feet and light a candle to you, because I cannot spoil anything so perfect."

His eyes as he looked at her seemed to be blazing with fire, and he went on very quietly:

"You said our love comes from God, and so do you. That is why I must leave you, and we must not come here again."

He bent once again over her hand, kissing it not passionately but very gently, as if she were infinitely precious.

Then before Zorina could speak, before she could prevent him from leaving her, he had melted into the shadows and she was alone.

She sat for a long time looking at the moon as the train sped on through the night.

*　　*　　*

From that moment until the end of the journey Zorina found there was no possibility of speaking to Rudolf, and somehow he contrived even to keep out of her sight.

When they stopped at a station, he was always first out of the train and, accompanied by an *Aide-de-camp*, he would disappear until it was time to reembark.

Then when they were in the Drawing-Room coach, he contrived to sit behind her so that she could not look at him.

His place was taken by the Foreign Secretary of Leothia, who was a dry, pompous man, and made everything he said sound exceedingly dull.

Because she realised what Rudolf was doing, Zorina spent a great deal of time in her sleeping-compartment.

"Are you all right, Dearest?" her mother asked anxiously.

"I have a slight headache, Mama, from the movement of the train, and I find it very difficult to concentrate on what people are saying."

"Then of course you must rest," her mother agreed. "The most important thing is for you to look lovely and feel well when we arrive."

Because she was frightened of what lay ahead, Zorina nearly answered that as far as she was concerned, the journey could go on forever.

She knew when she looked at him that Rudolf was feeling the strain.

He seemed paler than when he had come aboard, and only she would have noticed that there were lines under his eyes, which told her he was not sleeping.

She almost wished they could have a train smash.

Then, if she were dead, there would be no more problems, no more difficulties which seemed now to be insurmountable.

Perhaps because she was young and also had been taught to believe in the power of prayer, there was still a faint hope in her heart, like the light at the end of a tunnel.

By a miracle something might happen so that the future would not be as bad as she anticipated.

Nevertheless, as they travelled towards Archam, which was the Capital of Leothia, she could not help being thrilled by the countryside through which they passed.

As she had been told, Leothia was a small country, but there were high snow-topped mountains encircling most of its borders.

In the centre there was a fertile valley with a silver river running through it.

It was like a country out of a fairy-tale, with smiling peasants working in the fields yielding fertile crops or brilliant with flowers.

Sunshine illuminated the red roofs of the Alpine-style cottages.

There were Castles perched high on hills that seemed

to rise almost vertically out of the ground to be silhou-
etted against the blue sky.

"It is lovely!" Zorina exclaimed when the train
crossed the border from Austria.

She looked round as she spoke to see if Rudolf was
near her, wanting to share her enthusiasm with him.

But she could not see him and returned disappoin-
tedly to viewing the beauty of the land over which she
would reign.

When the train drew into the station at Archam, she
was aware before it came to a standstill that there was a
large welcoming party on the platform.

The station itself was decorated with flags, bunting,
and flowers.

A guard of soldiers in red and white uniforms and
their Commander in a plumed helmet were very impressive.

As the train came to a standstill, Rudolf came to
Zorina's side.

"Will you step out first, Your Royal Highness?" he
asked formally.

Without thinking, Zorina put out her gloved hand for
him to help her to her feet.

As his fingers closed over hers she felt as if a shaft of
light joined them and she knew he felt the same.

Then, as they walked towards the entrance to the carriage hand-in-hand, she felt her fingers squeezed almost
bloodless and knew how desperately he loved her.

Rudolf's brother, the Crown Prince Karl, greeted her
first.

There was some resemblance to Rudolf, but he
looked stiff, and there was a languid air about him that
Zorina had not expected.

He made her a formal speech of welcome and excused his father from being present, saying he was slightly indisposed.

"He will, however, Your Royal Highness, be waiting for you eagerly at the Palace," he said, "and now may I present my wife."

Looking at the Crown Princess, Zorina could understand why her husband looked somewhat dispirited.

She was a heavily-built, sharp-featured Princess of German origin.

They had been married, Zorina had already learned, by arrangement between their countries when they were both very young.

From the way the Crown Princess greeted her, Zorina knew there was no friendship for her there.

Next to be presented was the Lord Chamberlain, a cheerful man, and his wife, who was very smartly dressed but over-gushing in her aim to make Zorina feel welcome.

There were a few more introductions, followed by the two National Anthems, played slowly and pompously by a Regimental Band.

Then they proceeded out through the crowds that packed the inside of the station to where outside were waiting the State carriages to carry them to the Castle.

In the first one Zorina travelled with the Crown Prince.

In the second was her mother, the Crown Princess, Rudolf, and another Royal relative.

There were three carriages behind them, and Zorina was well aware that she should have been met and escorted by the King.

She wondered as she waved to the cheering crowds

whether he was really indisposed, or was there some ulterior motive in his not coming to greet her.

Then with an effort she forced herself to smile at the people along the rouge, and show them she appreciated the effort they were making.

There were Union Jacks everywhere, small ones waved by the children, large ones flying from buildings, and incorporated with the flag of Leothia on the lamp-posts.

It was impossible not to appreciate the picture the Leothians made in their native dress which Zorina knew was very much the same over the whole of the Balkans.

There was the full red skirt, the embroidered blouse, and black velvet corset.

For high days and holidays, of which this was one, on every woman's head a head-dress of coloured ribbons.

When they saw Zorina they obviously appreciated how young and pretty she was.

Her bonnet, decorated with Spring flowers, made her look, although she was not aware of it, like Persephone herself.

There were flowers everywhere, and bunches of them were thrown into the open carriage.

By the time they had passed through the main streets of the town and were climbing up the hill, Zorina and the Crown Prince seemed to be covered by a blanket of blossom.

It was then that Zorina had her first sight of the Palace.

It was perched high above the town, gleaming white in the sunshine and looking exactly as if it had stepped out of a fairy-tale book.

Its towers and turrets were gleaming, and the hill on which it stood was green with young trees, some of them in bloom.

It was so lovely that Zorina drew in her breath.

At the same time, she knew that if she had been driving there with Rudolf, it would have been a right and fitting end to the tale of their love.

Instead, the Palace was the cage in which she would be imprisoned with a husband she had not yet seen.

For some reason yet to be made clear he had made excuses not to be at the station to welcome her.

She had known when the Crown Prince was making his father's apologies that the reasons he gave for his absence were not the truth.

She could hear it in the dull tones in his voice, see it in the shifting of his eyes.

"What is . . . wrong?" Zorina wanted to ask.

Then, as the cheers of the crowd were left behind and the Palace loomed up ahead, she felt frightened.

She felt cold and she knew, too, that her hands were trembling.

chapter five

CLOSE, the Palace was even lovelier than it had appeared in the distance.

In front, there were wrought-iron gates surmounted by a crown, and every spike was tipped with gold.

Inside, there were fountains in sculptured stone basins throwing iridescent rainbows up into the sky.

The garden was a mass of brilliant flowers against a background of trees.

As the carriage came to a standstill at a long flight of marble steps, the Crown Prince said:

"I expect my father will be waiting for you at the door."

With an effort Zorina managed to flash him a smile, although she felt that there were a thousand butterflies fluttering in her breast.

Soldiers presented arms and she walked slowly beside the Crown Prince up the red-carpeted steps.

Because she was frightened, she was praying:

'Please, God, do not . . . let him be . . . horrible. Please, God, let me . . . like him.'

The Crown Prince moved slowly, and Zorina was aware that he was allowing time for the rest of the party from the other carriages to proceed behind them.

When they had almost reached the top of the steps, Zorina saw a man come out and, with a sinking of her heart, she thought it was the King.

He was wearing a uniform ablaze with decorations.

Zorina found it hard to look at his face but, before she could do so, the Crown Prince murmured:

"The Commander-in-Chief of the Army."

She looked at him in surprise, thinking it strange that the King was not waiting as his son had expected.

Then, as they met the Commander-in-Chief, he welcomed Zorina and burst into a flood of explanations as to why His Majesty was unfortunately not well enough to greet her, as he had intended to do.

"I suppose," the Crown Prince said, "that the Prime Minister and the other members of the Cabinet are waiting."

"They are all in the Throne Room, Your Royal Highness," the Commander-in-Chief replied, "together with the Ambassadors and a large number of other people who are extremely eager to meet Her Royal Highness."

"Let us get on with it," the Crown Prince said sharply.

He was speaking Leothian, but during her journey Zorina had managed to learn quite a lot of the language.

She was not yet very sure of herself when she spoke,

but she found it easy to understand what was being said to her.

Because she could not talk to Rudolf, and the Foreign Secretary was opposite her, she insisted on his talking to her in his own language.

She found to her delight that so many words were the same as those of the Balkan languages which she knew, and it was much easier to learn than she had expected.

As they walked down the passage, the Crown Prince said in a rather embarrassed voice:

"I am sure my father will be well enough to meet you this evening. We are having a family Dinner-party which I hope you will enjoy."

Zorina did not reply.

In a way, although it was strange, she was glad not to have to meet the King until she had time to see more of her surroundings.

The Palace was certainly very impressive and, she thought, unexpectedly beautiful.

There were many pictures that she wanted to look at closely. The furniture, much of which she suspected was the work of local craftsmen, was unusual and attractive.

Then they were in the Throne room which was exactly as she had expected.

There was a gold throne, under a canopy of crimson velvet, decorated with the Leothian arms.

The walls were covered in mirrors, and was a replica of Versailles. There were carved gold stands for the lights which Zorina thought would be dazzling when they were lit.

The ceiling was painted with a profusion of gods and goddesses of classical mythology.

The room itself was filled with what Zorina thought

must be all the dignitaries of Leothia, wearing their best on such an auspicious occasion.

The women were blazing with jewels, their bonnets fluttering with feathers which, with their bustles, made them look like birds of Paradise.

The men, not to be outdone, wore their decorations on uniforms which were as colourful as their wives' gowns.

There was silence as Zorina and the Crown Prince appeared in the doorway.

Then they moved along a narrow red carpet which led them directly to the dais on which stood the throne. Spontaneously everyone present began to clap.

Because it was so unexpected, Zorina found herself blushing and at the same time smiling.

When she and the Crown Prince stepped onto the dais, there was a surge forward from everyone in the room as if they wanted to see her more closely.

The Crown Prince made another stiff and boring speech of welcome, again excusing his father for his absence.

Then the presentations began.

The Lord Chamberlain announced who each person was as they climbed up one side of the dais, curtsied to the Crown Prince and Zorina, and descended on the other side.

The Prime Minister came first, then the members of the Cabinet, followed by the Ambassadors of every country which was represented in Leothia.

Because she thought it would surprise them, which it certainly did, Zorina spoke to each one of them in their own language.

She knew, as they expressed their astonishment, and

when she saw them whispering after they had left her, that they thought she was remarkable and were delighted.

It took a long time before the presentations were completed.

Then, without waiting for the Crown Prince to suggest it, she walked down from the dais into the room and moved around the guests.

She talked first to one and then to another.

After what seemed a very long time, Zorina and her mother were shown to their bed-rooms so that they could tidy themselves before luncheon.

"You were splendid, darling," the Princess said. "I was very proud of you."

She gave a little laugh before she said:

"You certainly astonished the Ambassadors. Each one of them came up to me to say how amazing it was that you could speak their language! And also that you are exactly the Queen Leothia needs."

"Did you discover what was wrong with the King?" Zorina asked because it was the thought which was uppermost in her mind.

She noticed that her mother's expression changed as she said quickly:

"I must go to my own room and wash. I am longing for something to eat, as I am sure you are."

She hurried from the room.

As she did so, a maid came in, curtsied, and said:

"I'm to look after Your Royal Highness and I hope that I'll give satisfaction."

She was a young woman of about twenty-five and, as she spoke slowly, Zorina understood.

"I am sure you will," she replied in Leothian with a smile.

The maid gave a cry of delight:

"Your Royal Highness speaks our language! That's good, very, very good."

"I speak a little," Zorina replied, "and you must help me to be really proficient."

"It's a great honour for me to help Your Royal Highness."

"What is your name?" Zorina enquired.

"It's Hildegard, Your Royal Highness."

"Then, Hildegard, you must help me," Zorina said. "You can imagine it is very difficult for me coming from so far away to live in a country I have never seen before."

It was a cry from one woman to another.

Hildegard clasped her hands together as she said:

"I pray to God that I can really help Your Royal Highness."

*　　*　　*

It was a huge Luncheon-party which, despite the excellent food and the beauty of the Dining-Room itself, Zorina found rather boring.

One after another the dignitaries present rose and made long and pompous speeches.

They expressed their admiration for Britain and Queen Victoria, their joy at having a Queen, not only with her British connection, but who was also connected with the part of Europe in which Leothia was situated.

When at last it seemed there was no-one else to make a speech, Zorina turned to the Crown Prince and asked:

"Shall I say thank you?"

He looked at her in astonishment, then replied a little grudgingly:

"If you think it necessary."

Zorina rose to her feet and saw the surprise in the eyes of the people looking at her.

Slowly, because she was not quite certain of her words, she said in Leothian:

"I am very grateful for all the kind things you have said and I promise you that I will do my best to be a good Queen. I already feel that no country could be more beautiful and no people so kind and welcoming."

She sat down and the applause, now spontaneous and unaffected, rang out, filling the great room from floor to ceiling.

The Crown Prince and Zorina led the way towards the door, still to triumphant applause.

They were now free, the Crown Prince said, to rest if they wished to be alone until it was time for dinner.

There was a private Sitting-Room attached to Zorina's bed-room which was, she thought, very lovely.

It was massed with flowers which scented the air, and she felt for the moment relaxed and unafraid.

"You were wonderful, Dearest," the Princess said. "You have certainly captured the hearts of everyone in Leothia. I know your father would have been very proud of you."

"I have not . . . yet seen . . . the King," Zorina said in a very small voice.

"They assure me that he will be well enough to be at dinner," the Princess replied.

Then, as if she wished to change the subject, she went to the window and exclaimed:

"I had no idea that Leothia was so beautiful. I

thought as we drove from the Station that the people looked happy and well-fed."

"I thought the same," Zorina replied. "The Foreign Secretary told me on the train that there was very little real poverty."

"I am sure you will be happy here," the Princess replied.

There was a note in her voice that made Zorina think she was really reassuring herself.

As she dressed for dinner with Hildegard's help, Zorina found herself once again feeling afraid of meeting the King.

Although she tried not to think of Rudolf, it had been impossible not to be aware that he was at the luncheon.

Her first thought at the applause following her speech was that he would think that she had done the right thing.

She had thought, too, as she walked up the steps, thinking the King would be at the top of them, that if only she were meeting Rudolf, it would be the happiest day of her life.

Every time she looked at the mountains, she would think of him climbing them.

When she saw the river winding through the fertile valley, and the fields full of flowers, Zorina thought she would like to ride through them with him beside her.

She knew that if she could do that, the land would really be enchanted.

'I love him . . . I love . . . him,' she thought as Hildegard brought one of her prettiest gowns from the wardrobe.

"Will your Royal Highness wear this tonight?" the maid asked.

"Yes, I like that gown," Zorina replied.

She was wondering if Rudolf would admire her in it and if there would be a chance of her speaking to him alone.

She had a feeling that he would keep very much in the background as he had done on the train, and avoid her as much as possible.

'How can he be so cruel, so unkind?' her heart cried out.

But her brain told her that he was doing the right thing.

"Your Royal Highness looks very, very beautiful," Hildegard was saying in an awed tone.

Zorina was suddenly aware that she was dressed and that her hair had been arranged. Because she had been thinking of Rudolf, she had been quite oblivious of this happening.

Now she looked in the mirror and knew, without being conceited, that Hildegard had spoken the truth.

She looked beautiful, and it was for a man who had not yet condescended to welcome his bride-to-be.

Zorina came out of her bed-room and crossed the corridor towards her mother's room.

Because she was in the Royal Suite, which she would occupy when she was Queen, her mother had been accommodated in a bed-room which was as near hers as possible.

It was not as grand as the one known as "The Queen's Room," but it was still very attractive. The furniture and pictures were all valuable works of art.

Zorina was just about to open her mother's door, when two Gentlemen appeared a little farther along the passage.

The King's suite, she had been told, was divided from the rest of the wing by two large and impressive doors painted in the eighteenth century.

They were surmounted by the Royal Coat of Arms in gold.

Both the Gentlemen who had come through them were in the evening-dress uniform of the Leothian Army.

As they stepped into the corridor and the doors shut behind them, they paused to speak to each other, obviously unaware that Zorina was only a little way from them.

"Is he all right?" one of the gentlemen enquired.

"Shall we say he is on his feet," the other replied.

"Then try and keep him on them."

They were both speaking Leothian.

As they started to walk along the passage, Zorina slipped quickly into her mother's bed-room without knocking, hoping that they had not seen her.

"I am nearly ready," the Princess said.

She was adjusting a tiara which she had borrowed before they left London.

Zorina did not speak. She was trying to puzzle out what she had heard about the King.

'Was he so ill that he could hardly stand? If so, surely it was a mistake for him to come down to dinner.'

Zorina only hoped that what he was suffering from was not infectious.

*　　*　　*

The dinner guests had assembled in a large Salon which adjoined the Dining-Room.

It also was a very beautiful room. Whilst Zorina was

talking to the guests who were already assembled, she learned that the entire Palace had been decorated by the King's mother.

She had been French and Zorina was told that she had exquisite taste. This was undoubtedly true.

There was no sign of Rudolf, although Zorina looked for him quickly as she entered the room.

Then, as they were awaiting the arrival of the King, Rudolf came in dressed as he had been at Windsor Castle.

Zorina felt as though the lights had suddenly flared up towards the ceiling and there was an aura around him that was dazzling.

Then, as he stopped to speak to someone just inside the door, because she was so closely attuned to him she knew perceptively that he was upset.

She could see that Rudolf's eyes were dark and stormy. He was not smiling, and his lips were set in a hard line.

She wanted desperately to go to his side.

She knew, however, that that was something which Rudolf would think was wrong, and with a great effort she started a long conversation with a very old man.

She gathered that he was a distant cousin who owned a huge Castle and estate in the north of the country.

It seemed as though everyone kept glancing at the door to see what was keeping the King.

Then two *Aides-de-Camp* came into the room and stood to attention at either side of the doorway.

The King appeared and, for a moment, it was impossible for Zorina to look at him.

She was afraid, desperately afraid, of what she would see.

She was aware, however, that everyone was moving quickly into two lines and that she stood alone with the King at the other end of the room.

This was the moment when they would meet.

Slowly, very slowly, she thought, he started to advance towards her until, when he was halfway down the room, she forced herself to raise her eyes.

Her first thought was that he was old, very old. Her second was that he was not the least what she had expected.

Because it made her feel better, she had vaguely imagined that the King would be an older version of Rudolf.

Now Zorina saw that the King was stout, which she had not expected, and his face was red—in startling contrast to his thinning white hair.

He had bushy, grey eye-brows and a large, rather untidy grey moustache.

The King came nearer still, and now he said in a voice which sounded unnecessarily loud:

"I must apologise, my dear young lady, for being such a tardy bridegroom. I am ashamed of myself, very ashamed. But, of course, you will forgive me."

He laughed, and somehow it sounded out of place and rather vulgar under the crystal chandeliers and in such a beautiful room.

Zorina curtsied.

The King took her hand and would have raised it to his lips, but for some reason he seemed to stagger.

Instantly one of the *Aides-de-Camp* was at his side, supporting him.

He raised his head:

"Dinner!" he exclaimed. "I expect you are all

hungry. I know I am. Come on, come on, what are we waiting for?"

The *Aide-de-Camp* whispered something in his ear.

"Yes, yes, of course," the King said.

He held out his arm to Zorina.

"I must not forget my bride, must I?"

His loud voice seemed to echo in the silence which had fallen upon the room.

Zorina took his arm and adjusted her pace to his.

As the King turned towards the door, the *Aide-de-Camp* on the other side was helping him.

Outside in the corridor the *Aide-de-Camp* was still beside them, and it flashed through Zorina's mind that perhaps the King had suffered a stroke of some sort.

That would explain why he was unsteady.

It was, however, difficult to think of anything except that he was old and not the sort of man she had expected to reign over such a lovely country.

'I must . . . try and . . . like him . . . I must,' she admonished herself.

Because Zorina shrank from being close to him, she was glad when they entered the Dining-Room and she realised that there was quite a gap between her chair and that of the King.

His was very impressive, carved in gilt with crimson velvet cushions and, Zorina thought, not unlike a throne.

Her chair was the same as all the other chairs around the table. She supposed it was because she was not yet Queen.

She felt herself shiver because she did not wish to think of the difference her marriage would make in little things as well as more important ones.

The King had not spoken to her since they had sat down.

The rest of the party were taking their seats and the King was having a *sotto voce* argument with one of the *Aides-de-Camp* who stood behind his chair.

Zorina's hearing was acute and, although the King had lowered his voice, she heard him say quite clearly:

"What the Devil do you mean? I want a drink and I am going to have one."

The *Aide-de-Camp*, in a much quieter voice, appeared to expostulate with him.

The King repeated:

"I am thirsty. I want a drink. If I do not have one, I shall leave."

The *Aide-de-Camp* obviously gave up the argument and a servant poured some wine into the King's glass.

He picked it up, drank it thirstily, and then, as the *Aide-de-Camp* once again whispered in his ear, the King said testily:

"Yes, yes, of course."

He swallowed some more wine before he said to Zorina:

"I drink your health, Princess, and welcome you to my country. I will say one thing, you are a very pretty girl—very pretty."

The King gave Zorina what she thought was almost a leering look, and she saw that his eyes were blood-shot.

Then he finished what remained in his glass and demanded that it be refilled.

Because she had been so bemused by what was happening on her left, Zorina had not realised that the Crown Prince was sitting on her right.

"Your father seems better," she said conversationally. "What has been wrong with him?"

There was a little pause before the Crown Prince replied:

"He has been slightly indisposed. I suspect he has been doing too much."

Zorina looked a little way beyond the Crown Prince and saw Rudolf.

She thought he was looking towards her and then realised that he was watching his father.

There was an expression of concern, and at the same time one of anger, in his eyes.

Zorina could tell, without words, that there was something wrong, very wrong, with the King.

As dinner commenced and course succeeded course, Zorina realised that the Crown Prince was deliberately holding her attention.

It was not difficult because the King was making no effort to talk to her and was concentrating on his food and drinking glass after glass of wine.

She was only able to glance at him, because the moment she turned her head, the Crown Prince said:

"Now there is something else I want to tell you which I know you will find interesting . . ."

He made everything he related sound dreary, and Zorina thought that perhaps he was unaccustomed to talking a great deal, as his wife had so much to say.

She could see the Crown Princess, who was at the end of the table.

She was talking German in a somewhat aggressive, domineering manner to the Commander of the Leothian Army, who was sitting on her right.

Zorina had been aware that before dinner the Crown

Princess had looked at her with an expression of dislike which was unmistakable.

'I cannot think why she should dislike me,' she thought, and then learned the reason.

As the Crown Prince paused for breath, Zorina said:

"Have you any children?"

There was a perceptible pause before he replied:

"Certainly, I have five daughters."

"Five!" Zorina exclaimed.

"I had always hoped for a son," the Crown Prince said dully, "but unfortunately my wife was very ill with our last child and now we cannot add to our family."

The way he had spoken told Zorina clearly what she thought she might have been told before.

The reason why the King wanted more children—and she shuddered at the idea—was that the Crown Prince had no heir and Rudolf was unmarried.

It was then that the reality of everything—which had seemed since they left the train like taking part in some theatrical performance—swept over her.

The King, this loud, red-faced man swilling down his wine beside her, was to be her husband because she was young and he wanted more sons to make sure of the succession.

Zorina wanted to rise in her chair and scream out to those seated round the table that she would not do it.

She wanted to walk out of the room and return to England.

'I will not . . . stay! I cannot . . . bear it! I have to go . . . I have . . . to,' she told herself.

Then her eyes met Rudolf's. She was aware that because he loved her, he knew what she was feeling.

They looked at each other. He was pleading with her, begging her not to make a scene.

Zorina wanted to defy him. She wanted to tell him that what was being asked was impossible.

There was a sudden crash beside her. Zorina turned to see what it was.

She realised that the noise had come from the King, but an *Aide-de-Camp* had pushed between her chair and his and she could not see what was happening.

Then, so quickly that some of the guests might not even have been aware of it, the two *Aides-de-Camp* took the King away.

Whether they were carrying him or he was walking between them, Zorina was not sure.

There was a door at the back through which they vanished with a swiftness which seemed incredible.

She was left staring in surprise. The King's chair beside her was empty.

A sudden hush spread over the assembled guests. Rudolf rose and walked from where he was sitting to take the King's chair next to Zorina.

It was as if his action were an order for everyone to behave as if nothing had happened.

They recommenced their conversations and the room was instantly filled with a buzz of sound.

"What has happened? Is your father ill?" Zorina asked.

Once again she thought that he might have had a stroke.

"He is not well," Rudolf said quickly. "But I want to tell you how lovely you are looking."

As he spoke, she was too intelligent not to realise that he was changing the subject.

Yet, because he was close beside her, because he was talking to her as he had refused to do on the train, Zorina felt that nothing else mattered.

He was there. He was near her and bending towards her.

She thought he was even more handsome than he had seemed the day before and the day before and the day before that.

"I love you," she wanted to say, and the King was forgotten.

Rudolf talked to her for the rest of the meal.

"Tell me what you think of my country now that you have seen it," he asked.

It was what Zorina had been longing to do.

She knew, as she answered his questions, that the words came into her mind like lines of poetry.

"And the Palace, is it what you expected?" he enquired.

"Far, far more beautiful."

"I wanted you to say that," he replied. "My grandmother, who altered it outside and completely decorated the inside, was a very remarkable person."

"You loved her?" Zorina asked.

"I not only loved her," Rudolf answered, "I have judged all the women I have met by her beauty and her standards."

Zorina knew, without Rudolf saying any more, that he thought she resembled his grandmother.

She felt a warmth within her which was very different from the fear which had consumed her earlier in the day and which now seemed to disappear.

"You are sleeping in the room which I insisted was

redecorated to be exactly as it was when my grand-mother was alive," Rudolf said.

Zorina realised that it must have been changed by the King's wife, and she answered:

"I will look at it more closely when I go upstairs."

"Also the Sitting-Room, where I used to go and talk to her when I was a little boy," Rudolf said. "She told me stories of the Greek goddesses who looked like you."

Zorina drew in her breath.

Rudolf went on quickly, as if he felt he had said too much:

"I ordered the flowers which I knew you would appreciate. To-night there will be orchids in your bed-room which have not been picked since my grandmother died."

"I am sure they...will be...beautiful," Zorina murmured.

"As beautiful as you," he said almost beneath his breath.

Because she was with Rudolf, it seemed only a few minutes before dinner was ended.

The Crown Princess rose to lead the Ladies from the Dining-Room.

As they reached the Salon where they had assembled before dinner, there was coffee and liqueurs waiting for them.

When the Gentlemen joined them, Zorina realised that everyone she spoke to was trying, without putting it into words, to apologise for the King.

They wanted to help her not to be upset by what had occurred at dinner.

It was not so much what they said in words, but she

could see the compassion in their eyes and feel it emanating from them in a way that could not be mistaken.

At the same time, no-one had actually mentioned the King by name, and this seemed so strange.

If he were really ill, surely they would be concerned about him and would ask if the Doctor had been sent for, and if so what was his verdict.

While they were at dinner, card-tables had been erected at one end of the Salon.

Quite a number of the older relatives started to play whist.

Zorina, however, to her overwhelming delight found that Rudolf was at her side.

She knew that if there had not been trouble, if the King had not been whisked away in that strange manner at dinner, he would in all probability not have come near her.

She knew that the other guests were thinking he was being tactful in keeping her amused, and she was determined to make the most of it.

"Please show me some of the treasures you have here and which were chosen by your grandmother," she begged.

Rudolf gave her a smile which made her heart turn several somersaults, and took her towards a glass case in which there was a collection of snuff-boxes.

This was at the other end of the room from those who were playing cards.

Zorina looked at the snuff-boxes when Rudolf had opened the case and realised that they were exceptional.

Decorated with diamonds and other precious stones, many of them contained a miniature in the centre.

Then, as she realised no-one could overhear what they said, Zorina asked softly:

"Have I . . . done what you . . . wanted me to . . . do so . . . far?"

"You have been marvellous—utterly and completely marvellous."

"You . . . liked my . . . speech?"

"Only you could have thought of thanking those present and have done it so perfectly."

"I wanted to . . . please . . . you."

"You were thinking of me?"

"It is . . . impossible for . . . me to . . . think of . . . anything else."

"Oh, my darling . . ."

He began a sentence and stopped. Zorina saw that the pain was back in his eyes.

"Please," she pleaded, "be kind to me. I am . . . frightened, very . . . frightened."

There was no need to elaborate that she was thinking of the King.

Zorina saw the frown between Rudolf's eyes, the hard line of his lips as he thought about his father.

"I know there is . . . nothing we can . . . do," Zorina said pathetically. "But . . . help me . . . please help me. Otherwise I cannot . . . go on."

"I knew that was what you were thinking at dinner," Rudolf said.

"Only . . . you would . . . understand," Zorina whispered. "And if you do not . . . help me . . . I shall . . . run away."

"I think you are blackmailing me," Rudolf said accusingly.

But his lips were smiling and now there was a twinkle in his eyes.

"I will blackmail you . . . kneel at your feet . . . or do . . . anything as long as . . . you do not . . . leave me . . . alone."

"Now you are thinking of yourself and not of me!"

He laughed, and it was a very tender sound before he went on:

"How can you look so absurdly beautiful, so untouched, so very childlike, and yet be so intelligent?"

"If I am . . . I think you are the . . . only person who would . . . appreciate it."

They were both aware that she was speaking of the King, and she saw Rudolf's fingers clench together as they rested on the side of the cabinet.

"It is intolerable," he said. "Absolutely intolerable!"

"But I can see . . . you and I can . . . talk . . . to you," Zorina said.

The positions seemed to be reversed.

Now she was comforting him, when she knew that he had set out to comfort her.

Rudolf did not need to speak, as his eyes were very eloquent.

"I love . . . you," Zorina said very softly, "and there is . . . nothing I can do . . . about it."

Rudolf just went on looking at her and, after a moment, she whispered:

"Promise . . . me that you will . . . not go . . . away. At least . . . not until after I am . . . married."

Her voice broke on the last word, and she looked down so that Rudolf would not see the tears in her eyes.

"I will stay," Rudolf said, and he spoke the words as if they were a vow, then he added:

"But only if God will give me the strength to endure it."

chapter six

WHEN she had finished her breakfast, Zorina found that
an *Aide-de-Camp* had left her a Programme for the day.

"I am afraid you are going to be very busy," Princess
Louise said as she had breakfast with her in the Sitting-
Room.

Zorina looked at the Programme and saw that she
was to receive three Deputations before luncheon.

Afterwards there was to be an inspection of the wedding-presents in one of the State-Rooms and then two
more Deputations later in the afternoon.

She thought, with a sinking of her heart, that these
would involve a great number of speeches which so far
she had found very dreary.

"You must not overtire yourself before to-morrow,"
her mother admonished her as she poured herself another cup of coffee.

"Why is to-morrow so particular?"

"Because you are to drive in State to the Houses of Parliament."

Zorina listened as her mother continued:

"We must choose one of your prettiest gowns because it will be the first time that the people in the City have seen you. Also the Members of Parliament will have a chance to admire you."

Princess Louise smiled as she spoke.

Zorina knew that her mother was deliberately trying to make the Programme seem attractive and she was well aware of the reason.

"Shall I be accompanied by the King?" she asked bluntly.

"Of course, Dearest," her mother said quickly, "I am sure he will be well by then."

She rose from the table, saying:

"I think you should hurry and get ready for the first Deputation which I believe is that of the Burgomasters."

Zorina had been right in thinking that the speeches would be long and dreary.

By luncheon time she was also tired of thanking the Deputations for the wedding-gifts they had presented with much ceremony.

As she had expected, there was no sign of the King, and the Crown Prince took his place.

Zorina had the feeling that a number of men in the Deputation looked at her with sympathy and expressions of compassion.

Luncheon was strictly a family meal and, to her joy, Rudolf was there.

The conversation, however, was monopolised by the Crown Princess.

One of her relatives, who was the reigning Grand Duke of a small Principality, had been attacked by an anarchist.

Although he was alive, he had lost an arm.

"It is disgraceful, utterly disgraceful, that nothing is done about these criminals," the Crown Princess kept saying in her strident voice, speaking in her own language in which it was easier for her to describe her feelings.

"There is very little that can be done," the Crown Prince said wearily. "No one has any idea who they are or where they are hiding—until they strike.'

"That is just the sort of thing you would say, Karl," his wife replied sharply. "It is just an excuse for the authorities to be lazy and do nothing."

The way she spoke was so offensive that Zorina stared at her in astonishment, thinking that the obvious animosity between husband and wife was very uncomfortable.

It struck her that perhaps in the future that was the way she would feel towards the King.

Once again she felt her fear of the future seep over her.

Rudolf looked at her across the table and she knew that he understood.

Somehow, because he was there and because she loved him, her panic slipped away.

She no longer listened to the Crown Princess ranting on and saying that it was just a question of proper organisation on the part of the Army and the Police.

Princess Louise brought luncheon to a welcome close, saying that as time was getting on, Zorina should have time to get ready for the inspection of the wedding-presents.

When they were alone going upstairs, Zorina said to her mother:

"How can the Crown Princess speak to Prince Karl so rudely in front of us?"

"She is a very tiresome woman," Princess Louise replied. "I am sure that her behaviour would shock Queen Victoria."

Zorina went to her own bed-room and, when she was ready, an *Aide-de-Camp* was waiting to escort her and Princess Louise downstairs.

The inspection of the wedding-presents was, she found, quite a ceremony.

They were accompanied by the Lord Chamberlain and several other Members of the Court, who explained to her in detail who had given each gift and its significance.

By the time they had finished, Zorina thought, although it seemed ungrateful, that she was no longer interested in large cups, bowls, salvers, and plates of gold or silver—all heavily inscribed.

She even found it impossible to be enthusiastic about the jewellery, which had been presented by the King's relatives.

Some of it was attractive, but she remembered she would have to wear it on State occasions with the King.

Once again Zorina was conscious of his red face and blood-shot eyes, and of the strange way he had behaved last night.

At last the exhausting day drew to a close and Princess Louise said:

"I think I would like to go upstairs and rest. I know

there is a Dinner-party to-night and I do not wish to disgrace myself by falling asleep."

Zorina laughed:

"It would be surprising! I, too, Mama, would like to rest."

"Then that is what we will do," her mother said.

They left the rest of the family, which included the Crown Princess. She had been obviously envious of the wedding-presents and was ready to disparage everything they had seen.

"You were very good, my Dearest," Princess Louise said as she and Zorina went upstairs. "Now try and sleep or read one of the interesting books which I have seen in the Sitting-Room."

Zorina knew that her mother was really suggesting, although she did not actually put it into words, that she should forget her wedding which would take place in three days' time.

Having seen her mother into her room, Zorina crossed the corridor towards her own bed-room.

She was actually turning the handle of her door, when a man dressed in Royal livery came hurrying up to her.

He stopped and spoke in a breathless tone:

"Excuse me, Your Royal Highness, but His Majesty wishes to receive you."

"His Majesty?" Zorina queried in surprise.

"Yes, Your Royal Highness, he's asked me to take you to him."

Zorina drew in her breath:

"Of course I will . . . come at . . . once."

She turned towards the end of the passage, where she

knew the King's Suite was situated, but the man beside her said:

"His Majesty's in his Private Apartments, Your Royal Highness."

Zorina looked surprised.

Then, as they walked in the other direction, the man said:

"I'm Josef, His Majesty's personal valet."

"You are taking me to His Majesty's Private Apartments?"

"Yes, Your Royal Highness. His Majesty uses the State-Rooms in this part of the Palace only on what you might call State occasions."

Zorina thought that the King's marriage was certainly a State occasion, but she made no comment.

Josef went on:

"His Majesty much prefers his rooms in the South wing, which is where I'm taking Your Royal Highness now."

They went on in silence, walking what seemed to Zorina to be a long distance before they descended a side staircase to the ground floor.

She realised by this time that they were at the other end of the Palace.

Josef walked towards an important-looking door and opened it.

Zorina's lips were dry, and there was a heavy feeling of frightened anticipation in her breast.

"Her Royal Highness, Princess Zorina," she heard Josef say.

Then she was inside the room and the door shut behind her.

A first glance told her that the room was quite different from those in the other parts of the Palace.

It seemed to her very ordinary and certainly less glamorous. She also saw that it was untidy.

Then Zorina could see or think of nothing except the King.

He was standing at the far end of the room by a cupboard which was open and the shelves were filled with bottles and glasses.

The King was holding a bottle and was pouring its contents into a glass which he held in his other hand.

He turned his head as she was announced and put down the bottle but kept the glass.

As she walked towards him, Zorina realised to her astonishment that he had removed his coat and was wearing a white shirt which was open at the neck.

His trousers were supported by braces.

Zorina was so surprised that she could only stare at him.

Because her father had been dead for years, she could not remember when she had last seen a man in shirt-sleeves.

"So, here you are," the King said as she advanced towards him.

Zorina curtsied.

"Your valet . . . told . . . me," she said in a hesitant little voice, "that Your Majesty . . . wished to . . . see me."

The King took a long drink and put down his glass.

"I have been told by my elder son," he said in a thick voice, "not only to see you, but to apologise for my behaviour last night."

Zorina could not look at him, but she managed to say:

"No . . . please . . . it is quite . . . unnecessary."

"He seemed to think it very necessary," the King replied. "Also that I should tell you how attractive I find you."

Zorina was looking down at the floor, feeling that this was very embarrassing and wishing that Prince Karl had not interfered.

She was also palpitatingly aware that she was alone with the King and that it was very difficult to control her feelings for him.

"You are very pretty," she heard him say. "It is true that I am a lucky man."

There was a note in his voice which made Zorina feel frightened.

Before she could express it even to herself, the King stepped forward and—to her utter astonishment—his arms went around her.

"Very pretty," he said thickly, "and you will give me the children I want."

His arms tightened. Zorina gave a scream as she realised that he was about to kiss her.

Instinctively she struggled so that the King's mouth touched the side of her cheek whilst his thick moustache was against her lips.

Zorina was aware of the strong smell of spirits, and every instinct in her body revolted against him and what he was doing to her.

She pressed her hands, fingers outstretched, against his chest, saying incoherently:

"No . . . no . . . let me go!"

The King, however, was stronger than she thought he would be. His arms held her closer. She could feel his lips hot against her skin.

Zorina threw back her head and at the same time she pushed him away from her.

She must have taken him by surprise, for his arms slackened a little and she thrust against him with all her strength.

The King moved as if to prevent her and, in doing so, fell backwards, crashing down on the floor and hitting his head against the carved corner of a seat of a chair.

He gave a groan, which was almost a cry, then his eyes closed and he did not move.

Shocked into immobility, Zorina stood staring at him, finding it hard to believe that it had actually happened and that the King was lying at her feet.

Then the door at the far end of the room opened and a woman came running down the room. She was red-haired and appeared to be nearing middle-age.

Zorina thought she must be a servant until she realised that she was dressed in a floating *négligée* of silk and lace.

The woman went down on her knees beside the King, putting one hand on his forehead and the other on his heart.

"I . . . am . . . sorry," Zorina began to say.

"Why did you knock him about like that?" the woman demanded furiously.

She spoke Hungarian, and Zorina could understand and answer in the same language.

"I am . . . very . . . sorry. I did not . . . mean to . . . hurt him."

"Well, you've knocked him out, that's what you've done."

"I did . . . not mean . . . to do so."

"You are going to be his Queen and that should be enough for you," the woman snapped. "You keep to your part of the Palace and do not come barging in here where he belongs to me."

"Belongs . . . to . . . you?"

"If nobody has told you, you might as well know the truth," the woman retorted. "We have lived together as man and wife for the last twelve years. I wouldn't give him up to the last Queen, and you're not having him now."

Zorina could only stare at her, feeling that what she was saying could not be true.

"You can have his children, which is what they are all fussing about," the woman went on. "I have given him three sons, so there is nothing wrong with him. Not like his son, Karl, who can produce only girls."

The woman was spitting out the words contemptuously.

She paused to look down at the King and then slipped her hand inside his shirt to rub his heart.

In a voice which Zorina did not recognise as her own she asked:

"Did you say that the King had given you three sons?"

"I did, and fine boys they are too," the woman replied. "And there's another one on the way."

She withdrew her hand from the King's shirt and said:

"There is no point in your standing there gaping. You've done enough damage, so get out and leave him to me. Don't you come down here again, do you understand?"

Zorina gave a gasp, then turned and ran to the door.

125

As she reached it, she realised that Josef had come into the room by the same way as the woman had.

She knew that he would tend to the King, and quickly she opened the door in front of her. The passage was empty.

By instinct Zorina found the staircase which she and Josef had used and she hurried up to the first floor.

Then she ran as quickly as she could to her own bed-room.

She went to the wardrobe and took from it the cape in which she had travelled on the ship which had carried her to Ostend.

She put it round her shoulders. Then she snatched from a drawer a chiffon scarf with which she covered her head, pulling it forward to conceal her face.

Leaving her room, Zorina went a little way back the way she had come, and found a staircase she had been told led down to the garden.

There was no-one about and again, largely by instinct because her brain had ceased to function, Zorina found the door into the garden and let herself out.

It seemed then that she knew where she was going and what she intended to do.

The trees were already casting long shadows and the sun was sinking behind the mountains as she walked until she found herself at the West Gate of the Palace.

Among the wedding-presents had been a gift from the Master Bakers of the City who had modelled in sugar a replica of the Palace and its gardens.

The Master Baker had laboriously pointed out to her the entrances. Indicating the West Gate, he had said:

"I am sure Your Royal Highness will be taken

through this Gate to view the Falls which are very famous."

"That is true," the Crown Prince remarked, "and also very beautiful."

The Master Baker went on:

"The Falls were there before the Palace itself was built. The water comes from some hidden stream in the mountain and falls hundreds of feet into a lake in the valley below."

His voice had been proud as he said:

"It is the most magnificent sight in Leothia and will, I am sure, delight Your Royal Highness."

"I am sure it will," Zorina had agreed.

She knew now that that was where she must go.

As she reached the West Gate, she pulled her cloak around her so that her white gown was hidden and bent her head to hide as much of her face as possible.

The sentries paid no attention to her.

They were talking together at the side of the Gate, which Zorina thought could not be in frequent use.

She started along a dusty lane which, a little farther on, petered out into a path running between olive trees.

She heard the sound of water and knew that the Falls were not far away.

The path made it easy for her to reach them. They were, as the Master Baker had said, magnificent.

The water rushed tempestuously in a silver torrent down the bare mountainside.

Far below, Zorina could see the beginning of the lake into which the water was falling.

It stretched out for some distance, and she thought, although she was not sure, that on the far side there were bathing huts.

From what she could see, looking down through the spray, below her there was no sign of human habitation.

'I shall be dead when I touch the water,' Zorina told herself.

There was a rock jutting out of the ground.

She sat down on it, thinking that she would wait a little just in case there was anyone in the vicinity who might be so foolish as to rescue her.

'I will fall in my cloak,' she thought 'then, if my body is found, they will believe it was an accident.'

She had begun now to think clearly.

The horror of the King's attempted kiss and the manner in which he had fallen was still vivid.

Zorina knew that the shock which she had experienced at first was gradually wearing off.

Now she understood that he drank, which she had been too ignorant to realise before.

She was sure it had not been his wish to marry again and have more children, but perhaps that of the Prime Minister and senior members of the Cabinet.

"Why should the King himself want another wife," she asked herself, "when he had that strange Hungarian woman and her sons?"

Zorina's mind still shrank from the knowledge that the woman was having yet another child by the King, when it was intended that he should be her husband.

'How can they expect me to do anything so horrible, so degrading, as to marry him?" Zorina asked.

She was too intelligent not to know the answer.

As far as Leothia was concerned, all that mattered was that there should be heirs to the throne to help to maintain its independence.

"I cannot do it," Zorina told herself. "It is far, far easier to die."

She felt as if the Falls were hypnotising her.

The last rays of the sun were turning the water to gold, then it was crimson, as though it ran with blood.

She thought she would be buried with glory, and perhaps, when he learned what had happened, Rudolf, if no-one else, would understand.

'The sooner I die, the better,' she decided.

She was half afraid that, at the last moment, she would shrink from what had to be done.

Or worse still, someone might find her and she would be taken back to the Palace.

She felt a sudden panic in case that should happen.

How could she go back to be the wife of a man who drank, a man who was already married in everything but name to a woman who obviously cared for him?

Zorina felt again the revulsion she had experienced when he had tried to kiss her.

She felt his moustache brush her lips as he held her in his arms, dressed in an open-necked white shirt.

It all seemed so coarse, so degrading, and utterly humiliating.

How could she allow such a man to touch her?

The idea of bearing his child was so revolting that she dared not even think of it.

"I must die quickly," she whispered.

If they took her back, she might never be able to escape again.

Zorina rose from the rock on which she had been sitting and moved a few steps nearer to the Falls.

The water was only a few inches away, and she realised that if she flung herself forward, she would be carried instantly and forcefully down to be dashed to death on the rocks.

If, by some miracle, she survived that, she would be unconscious by the time she drowned in the Lake itself.

It seemed so simple, so easy, and she knew that if there were a life after death, her father would be waiting for her and she would not be alone.

'Help me . . . Papa. Help . . . me,' she prayed.

Zorina felt as if she could see her father and that he was smiling at her as he had when she was a child.

She took a deep breath and put out her hands as though to protect her face from her first impact with the water.

Then she gave a scream as from behind she was pulled back violently from the edge of the Falls.

She experienced a moment of terror. Then there were two arms around her and a deep voice was saying:

"My darling, my sweet, how could you do anything so wicked? How could you leave me?"

For a moment Zorina could not breathe.

Then, as Rudolf's lips took possession of her, she felt as if the whole world had exploded into a dazzling light.

He was kissing her, kissing her fiercely, demandingly, possessively, until it was impossible to think of anything except that he was there and that she was his —completely and utterly his.

An eternity passed before Rudolf raised his head to say:

"I love you, oh, God, how I love you!"

The words seemed to seep into Zorina's consciousness.

Then he was kissing her again, not so fiercely, but with slow, demanding, passionate kisses.

She felt as if he drew her heart from her body, and also her very soul.

As she moved a little nearer to him, Zorina knew that she was merged entirely in him. She was his and there was no life apart from him.

Then, as Rudolf looked down at her, she gave a cry of sheer agony as she said:

"I . . . cannot go . . . back. I will . . . not go . . . back. Please . . . let me . . . die."

"Do you really think I would lose you?"

"You do . . . not . . . understand . . . you cannot . . . understand."

"I do understand, my darling. I know now that it is impossible for you to do what has been asked of you."

"You realise . . . that?" Zorina asked doubtfully.

Rudolf did not speak.

"You knew . . . you knew what . . . he was . . . like . . . and the children he had . . . by that . . . woman. How could . . . you ask me to . . . marry him?"

Her voice broke on the words and she hid her face against Rudolf's neck.

He held her close and said:

"The Statesmen were all convinced that an English Queen was what the country needed."

His lips were against her forehead as he went on:

"How was I to know, how was I to guess, that the little goddess I fell in love with the moment I saw her would be the woman who had been chosen for my father?"

"I . . . cannot go . . . back," Zorina murmured, as if any explanation would be superfluous.

"I know that," Rudolf replied. "I am taking you away."

She lifted her head to look at him.

"Where are . . . you taking . . . me?"

He looked at her as if he had never seen her before and must imprint her beauty on his mind. Then he said:

"Are you brave enough, my darling, to cause a scandal which will mean that we shall both be exiled—from my country and from yours?"

"I will . . . do anything . . . anything in the . . . world as . . . long as I can be . . . with you."

Rudolf smiled, and his eyes were very tender.

"In that case, there are no problems. Come, the sooner we get away, the better."

He held her closely and kissed her.

Now it was a very gentle kiss—a kiss of dedication.

Zorina had no clear idea what was happening, but it did not matter, nothing mattered except that she was with Rudolf and he did not intend to take her back to the Palace.

They went a little way along the path by which she had come, and she saw his horse quietly eating the grass under the trees.

"I had just arrived back to the Palace," Rudolf explained, "when one of the *Aides-de-Camp,* who is a friend of mine, told me he had learned that my father's valet had taken you without their permission to see the King."

"He . . . sent for . . . me," Zorina murmured.

"I arrived a few minutes after you had left. My father had just recovered consciousness and I learned what had happened."

Rudolf's voice was hard and Zorina was aware how angry it had made him.

"I went to your room to find you," he went on, "and Hildegard told me that you were not there. But the wardrobe was open and your cape was missing."

"You . . . guessed where I . . . had gone?"

"I think, my darling," Rudolf replied as he lifted her onto the saddle of his horse, "that my intuition as far as you are concerned is very acute. I was desperately afraid that you would come here."

"I . . . meant to . . . die . . ."

"I knew that as soon as I saw you. I thank God in His mercy that I was in time."

Rudolf sprang into the saddle behind her.

He held her closely against him with his left arm, his reins in the other hand, and started to ride down the side of the hill.

It was steep, but he zig-zagged between the trees. Then they were in the valley and he could move faster.

The sun had sunk, leaving only a glow in the sky. The peasants had already left the fields.

Lights were beginning to shine from the windows of the small houses which they passed.

Zorina felt as if she had stepped into a dream, but whilst she was dreaming she was acutely conscious that she was close to Rudolf.

It was a sensation of security she had longed for and made her feel as if she were floating among the clouds.

Almost as if she had asked a question, Rudolf said:

"I love you, my darling, and whatever difficulties we may face, we shall be together and supremely happy."

"I love you . . . so overwhelmingly," Zorina whispered, "That was why it was . . . easier to . . . die than to live . . . without you."

Rudolf let his lips touch her head. She felt as if lightning swept through her body, and her whole being thrilled.

It was so intense and so wonderful that she could only put her cheek against his shoulder and thank God that she was with him.

They rode for quite a long way before Rudolf turned off the dusty track and started to make his way among the trees.

"Where . . . are we . . . going?" Zorina asked.

"To be married."

She looked at him in astonishment.

"Now . . . this moment?"

"There will be no more arguments, no more decisions to make after that. You will be my wife and no-one shall take you from me."

"Oh . . . Rudolf . . ."

Tears came into Zorina's eyes and then, resolutely, because she knew she must say it, she asked:

"Are you . . . quite sure? Are you certain that you can bear having caused a . . . scandal and being . . . exiled from your own . . . country?"

She went on quickly:

"I am . . . unimportant. No-one worried about me until Queen Victoria told me to . . . marry your . . . father. You are . . . different . . . you are . . . important to . . . Leothia."

"Nothing is important except that you should be mine," Rudolf answered.

"Supposing you . . . regret . . . marrying . . . me?" Zorina asked in a very small voice.

"Loving you will be the most perfect, glorious thing which could ever happen."

"That is . . . different."

"There is no difference," he said. "We want each other, we need each other. We cannot live without each other. It is something I should have recognised before now."

As Rudolf spoke he drew his horse to a standstill, and Zorina saw that there was a small building in front of them.

It was fashioned out of tree-trunks and yet, before she saw the Cross over the doors, Zorina realised that it was a Church.

Rudolf smiled at the astonishment in her eyes. Then he dismounted and lifted her down from the saddle:

"My precious, I am taking you to meet the man who has always been a good friend to me and whom I admire more than anyone else I have ever met."

He left his horse loose and, taking Zorina by the hand, led her up three wooden steps and through the door, which was ajar.

Inside was the strangest Church which Zorina had ever seen.

There were pillars made from whole trees and the walls were carved and painted with the expert craftsmanship which was to be found all over the Balkans.

She wanted to look, but Rudolf drew her forward and she saw, kneeling in front of the Altar at the other end of the Church, a man with white hair wearing a Monk's robe.

He was praying.

Then, as if he were aware that they were standing behind him, he crossed himself and rose to his feet.

Rudolf released Zorina's hand and moved forward to kneel in front of the Priest.

He put his hand on Rudolf's bare head and said:

"It is good to see you, my son."

"And I have missed you, Father," Rudolf said. "Now I need your help."

"You know that is what I am here for," the Priest replied.

Rudolf rose to his feet.

"I am asking you to marry me, Father, to someone I love and who was meant by God to be my wife."

He put out his hand as he spoke and drew Zorina forward.

The Priest seemed to Zorina to look deep into her soul before he said:

"Nothing would give me greater pleasure than to unite you both in the Sacrament of Marriage."

"I knew that was what you would say," Rudolf replied.

The Priest moved to the side of the Altar to put on an exquisitely embroidered Vestment which was laid on a chair.

As he did so, Rudolf undid the cape which Zorina was wearing and, taking it from her, laid it on one of the carved pews.

Then he loosened the white chiffon scarf which she wore over her head and round her neck.

As it fell over her shoulder and her white dress, she knew that Rudolf thought of it as a wedding veil.

The Priest wearing his Vestment, and on his head, to Zorina's surprise, the red Cap of a Cardinal, moved to stand in front of them.

Without a book he started the beautiful words of the Wedding Ceremony in Latin.

The Church seemed filled with the voices of the angels and, as Rudolf held her hand in his, Zorina knew that this was what she had longed for.

The love that they had for each other could have come only from God.

She prayed that she might make him happy and that he would never regret giving up so much for her.

She prayed, too, that Leothia would not suffer because she had run away and that they would find a Queen to take her place.

As the Priest blessed them, she knew, although it might seem wrong from a worldly point of view, that they were doing what was right in the eyes of God.

The Priest laid his hands on their heads and Zorina felt as if a light blazed round them and through their bodies.

Then he knelt down in front of the Altar, and Rudolf and Zorina both knew that he was continuing the prayers he had been saying when they arrived.

They looked at each other and Rudolf thought he had never seen anyone look so happy, so radiant, or so spiritual as his wife.

He helped Zorina to her feet and they left the little Church holding hands.

It was only when they were once again riding through the trees that Zorina said, almost in a whisper:

"That is . . . how I . . . wanted to be . . . married."

"I knew you would feel like that," Rudolf replied. "Father Augustine was a Cardinal, a great Prince of the Church, before he retired to worship God in his own way—in the forest among the animals and birds who trust him and come to him when they are wounded or hungry."

"How wonderful!" Zorina exclaimed.

"A few people, like myself," Rudolf finished, "are privileged to be his friends."

"I felt that . . . God really . . . did bless . . . us."

"That is what I felt too," Rudolf told her. "We think alike, we are alike, and now, my darling, we are one person."

He kissed her lips very gently, as if the sanctity of what they had just experienced had made them both spiritual rather than human.

When they had ridden for a little while in silence, Zorina asked:

"Where are we going?"

"To a secret hiding-place," Rudolf replied. "It belongs to a friend of mine who has gone to Greece on a holiday. He lends it to me whenever I need it. I think it is a perfect place in which to start our honeymoon."

"Any . . . place would be . . . perfect with . . . you," Zorina whispered.

As they rode on she thought she could feel his heart beating.

Half-way up the mountain they came to a small wooden house where Rudolf told her he had often hidden before.

"When I thought I could not stand the Palace any longer," he said, "and my father and my sister-in-law became intolerable, I wanted to run away."

"I can . . . understand . . . your feeling like . . . that."

He smiled before he replied:

"You are not to think of the past anymore. What we are concerned with is the future. Here, my beautiful, precious little bride, we start a new chapter of our lives and it is going to be a very exciting one."

Zorina looked back at the valley. The view was quite different from that from the Palace.

Here she could see more clearly the whole range of snow-capped mountains and the river winding through verdant fields.

The mountains held the last light of the day, and overhead the first evening stars were coming out.

Inside, Rudolf had already lighted the logs in the big, open fireplace.

On the floor were fur rugs made from the skins of wolves and bears which had been shot in the mountains.

On the wooden walls there were stags' antlers and some very skilfully painted pictures of the mountains.

There was a deep comfortable sofa and large arm-chairs, besides a table of polished wood and dressers which contained the brightly coloured plates and cups that were made by the country folk.

Rudolf drew Zorina across the room into the bed-room. For a moment she did not think it was real.

The Sitting-Room had been attractive in its own way, but the bed-room was lovely.

Someone with imagination had carved the bedhead with all the flowers to be found in the valley and had painted them in their natural colours.

The walls were painted white and the rugs on the floor were of lambswool and were white too.

There were velvet curtains over the windows which echoed the blue of the sky.

The whole room was so lovely that Zorina thought it might have been designed especially for her.

Rudolf read her thoughts:

"When I have stayed here in the past, I have always felt lonely in this room. I know now that I was missing you."

"Oh, darling . . . I am here . . . now."

"Do you suppose that I do not realise that?" he asked.

He pulled her into his arms and then he was kissing her fiercely, passionately, possessively—as if he would woo her and conquer her at the same time.

Then he said with what she thought was a superhuman effort:

"Before I love you as I want to do, I must give you something to eat. I think, perhaps, it will be sparse fare to-night, but to-morrow you shall be properly fed."

Zorina laughed because she knew that nothing mattered except that she was with Rudolf.

Because they were so happy, whether they ate or did not eat, they would be like the gods living on ambrosia.

Later, she tried to remember what they had eaten.

She knew there had been biscuits and honey in the cupboard and there had been fragrant coffee to drink.

Whatever it had been, it had tasted delicious because she was looking into Rudolf's eyes and listening to Rudolf's voice.

Her lips were ready for his kisses.

Afterwards he gave her a pitcher of water in which to wash and went outside to fetch logs for the fire in the bed-room.

As soon as he had gone Zorina undressed and got into bed, shy because she was wearing only her chemise.

Rudolf came into the room, put down the logs which

he was carrying, and looked at her in the light from the candle by the bedside.

The coloured flowers behind her, with her hair falling over her bare shoulders, made Zorina look ethereal.

She was like a sprite from the snows who had strayed by mistake down from the peaks above them.

"You know I love you," he said in his deep voice.

"And I . . . love . . . you."

She felt her heart beating frantically in her breast as he came towards her and sat down on the bed.

He took her hands in his and, as he felt her fingers quiver, he asked:

"You are not afraid, my darling?"

"Of you? How could I . . . ever be . . . afraid of . . . you? You are everything that means . . . safety and . . . security . . . love and happiness."

Her voice had a little note of passion in it and then she said in a different tone:

"I am only . . . afraid of . . . one . . . thing."

"What is that?"

"That you will be . . . disappointed in . . . me and feel perhaps . . . because I am . . . dull and . . . inexperienced that . . . you should not have . . . run away with me."

"Do you really think that I could ever regret anything that we have done?" Rudolf answered.

He bent down to kiss her, and then he blew out the candle beside the bed and pulled back the curtains.

Outside, Zorina could see the stars glowing like diamonds in the darkness of the sky.

There was only a small glimmer from the fire which Rudolf had just lit.

Then, as she waited, feeling a wild excitement rising within her which was different from anything she had ever known before, Rudolf was beside her.

She felt the strength of his body against the softness of hers.

As he took her lips captive, she thought:

'It is . . . impossible to be . . . alive and to know such . . . rapture.'

As his hands touched her body and he kissed her neck and then her breasts, Zorina thought it could not be true to feel the ecstasy he gave her.

It was as if he were carrying her up to the white peaks of the mountains and then into the dazzling light of the stars.

When Rudolph made her his, Zorina knew they were with God and part of God and their love was divine for all Eternity.

chapter seven

ZORINA was dreaming that Rudolf was kissing her, and she opened her eyes to find that he was.

He was sitting on the side of the bed and the sunshine was coming through the window, making the room glow with a golden light.

"You look very beautiful in the morning, my darling."

"I love you . . . I love . . . you," Zorina answered.

"And I love you," Rudolf replied. "But I am sure that you are hungry, and I have been to get your breakfast."

She looked at him and realised that he was dressed, although he was not wearing a coat.

It flashed through her mind that the last man she had seen in shirt-sleeves was the King.

Quickly she swept the memory away as she put her

arms around Rudolf's neck and pulled his head down to hers.

"Last . . . night was so . . . wonderful," she whispered.

"I did not hurt or frighten you, my darling?"

"I felt that we were . . . both in the . . . sky above the . . . mountain peaks."

He kissed her gently, as if she were infinitely precious, and said:

"I will go and cook your eggs for you and then we can talk about ourselves."

Zorina gave a little cry:

"I must . . . do that."

"I expect that I am a better cook than you are." Rudolf smiled and went from the room.

Zorina jumped up, washed in cold water which still had a touch of snow about it, and put on her clothes.

For the first time she realised that all she had was the dress that she was wearing when she ran to the Falls.

She wondered how she could obtain anything else.

Yet why should she worry about clothes when she could be with Rudolf?

When she went into the Sitting-Room she saw that he had laid the table. He was bringing from the kitchen a pan in which he had fried the eggs.

"I told you I would do that," Zorina protested. "I am sure it is quite . . . wrong for a . . . Royal Prince to . . . demean himself."

She was teasing, but he answered quite seriously:

"I am no longer a Royal Prince. I am plain Herr Rudolf and you, my darling, will have to choose an ordinary name by which we will be known in future."

Just for a moment Zorina regretted, because he

looked so much like a Prince, that he would no longer be one.

Then she said:

"None of that matters . . . except that . . . we will be . . . together."

"That is what I wanted you to say."

He fetched the coffee from the kitchen, together with a small loaf of newly baked bread, a pat of golden butter and—to Zorina's delight—a basket in which there was a number of different fruits.

"Where did all this come from? she asked. "Or did it materialise by magic!"

"The woman who looks after this house for my friend lives a little way down the mountain," Rudolf replied. "She was most annoyed that we had not let her know we were coming."

He paused and then continued:

"But I thought, last night, that it was wonderful for us to be alone."

"That is . . . what I . . . wanted . . . too."

Zorina sat down at the table, and she thought nothing could be more marvellous than to be in this tiny wooden house with Rudolf.

It was, to her, more beautiful and more glamorous than any Palace could be.

As if he knew what she was thinking, Rudolf said:

"That's what I feel too. But, my darling, we shall have to decide where we will go and where we shall live."

"I feel a little . . . guilty about . . . Mama," Zorina said in a low voice.

"As soon as we have left Leothia, you can write to her and tell her that we are safe and happy."

He paused before he went on:

"I would be surprised if she does not guess, when we are both missing, that I am looking after you."

"I hope she . . . will think . . . that."

Then, in the frightened little voice he knew so well, Zorina asked:

"If anyone . . . finds us here . . . will we be . . . arrested?"

Rudolf made a gesture with his hands which was very explicit.

"I do not know," he said. "It is possible that my father is feeling insulted and vindictive because you have run away. But I doubt if he will exert himself."

"Then . . . whom have we to . . . fear?" Zorina asked.

"I do not exactly know," Rudolf replied. "It was the Prime Minister who was most insistent that my father should take an English wife. The Members of the Court were, I think, against it."

"They must all have been . . . aware of the . . . way he was . . . living," Zorina said hesitantly.

"Of course they knew about Maria and his children," Rudolf replied, "but they thought it was quite immaterial politically."

As he spoke of it so easily and without embarrassment, Zorina felt some of the horror and disgust she had known slip away from her.

She was intelligent enough to realise that it had been such a shock because she had never imagined that any Gentleman, let alone a King, would behave in such a manner.

She had, in fact, been stunned when she learned the truth.

Rudolf was watching her, and her eyes were very revealing:

"I suppose," she said in a trembling voice, "that I was very . . . foolish and I should really be . . . ashamed of what I . . . did."

Rudolf took her hand and kissed it:

"I adore you, my precious, because you are innocent and completely unspoiled by the world. But it was wicked and wrong of you to think of taking your life."

He paused and then went on:

"Yet I think it made us both aware that we could no longer go on pretending that we could live without each other."

The way he spoke was very moving, and Zorina replied almost fiercely:

"That is true . . . I cannot . . . live without . . . you. If they take you . . . away from me . . . I swear I will . . . die."

He rose to pull her into his arms.

Then he was kissing her passionately, insistently, demandingly, as if he were still afraid that he might have lost her.

*   *   *

A long time later, when the sun was high in the sky and it was very hot, Rudolf kissed Zorina and said:

"Now we are both going to get up and catch our luncheon."

Zorina looked at him in surprise and he explained:

"It is something I have often done before. The blue trout in the stream outside are, I assure you, delicious."

Zorina laughed from sheer happiness.

"You are always thinking about food," she teased

him, "while I just want to stay here in this lovely warm room and only . . . think about . . . love."

"Do you imagine that I think of anything else," Rudolf asked in a deep voice.

He kissed her bare shoulder and then stroked her red-gold hair as it fell over the pillow.

"If you have thrown away all my hair-pins," Zorina said, "I shall have to walk about with my hair down, and you know that I have only one gown to wear."

It lay at the moment on the floor, where Rudolf had thrown it when he had undressed her and carried her back to bed.

"I shall have to find you some more clothes," Rudolf said. "Although Frau Toger can provide us with eggs and other food we need, I doubt if she can lend you a trousseau, as she is very large and fat!"

Just for a moment Zorina remembered the elegant gowns which were hanging in her wardrobes at the Palace and which she had been given by Queen Victoria.

Then she knew that she wanted them only so Rudolf would think that she looked lovely. Otherwise they were completely unimportant.

"Personally, I adore you just as you are," he was saying, caressing the softness of her body.

"I shall be cold when the sun goes down." Zorina laughed.

"Not if you are in my arms, as you will be," Rudolf answered.

Then he was kissing her breasts and she felt the ecstasy that his lips always gave her, rising until it became an inexpressible rapture.

Once again they were flying towards the mountain

peaks, and the sunshine burned like flames within them until they were utterly consumed by it.

* * *

"You have caught one!" Zorina exclaimed excitedly.

The fish fought against Rudolf's line while he pulled it relentlessly towards the net which Zorina held in her hands.

She landed it competently by the side of the mountain-spring and, when Rudolf had caught three more trout, they carried them back to the little house in triumph.

Zorina had learnt now that Rudolf's friend, Bernard, who owned it, was decorating it himself for the girl he was going to marry in six months' time.

"Why so long?" Zorina asked.

"Her father was insistent on a long engagement in case either of them change their mind."

"As it is decorated with love," Zorina said, "I feel sure that that is something she will never do. But I had no chance to change mine."

"Would you want to?" Rudolf asked.

Zorina put her arms around his neck.

"I cannot think now why you kept me waiting so long before you . . . carried me . . . away."

She laid her cheek against his as she said:

"To me, you are just like the Knight in the fairy-stories who rescues the Princess from the Dragon. And they live happily ever after."

"That is exactly what we are going to do."

Zorina moved a little closer to him:

"There is something I . . . want to . . . say to you."

"What is it?"

"Although, as you know, I have no money," Zorina said, "and you may have to leave yours behind in Leothia . . . I shall still be ecstatically . . . happy with you . . . wherever we . . . may be."

Before Rudolf could say anything, she went on:

"If it is nothing but a cave or a tent, and I have to work to provide for us both, and perhaps our children, I shall still thank God . . . every day that I am . . . your wife . . . the luckiest woman in . . . the whole world."

What she had said had come from the very depths of her heart and she knew that Rudolf was very touched by it as he kissed her gently and tenderly.

It was as if it were easier to express himself with kisses than with words.

* * *

They laughed a great deal over their luncheon, which was delicious, and then they lay in the shade because the sun was too hot.

They looked at the beauty around and above them.

The only sound came from the stream as it cascaded down into the valley.

Later in the afternoon they talked of many things, not only themselves, but Rudolf told her of places he had visited in the world,

He found that although Zorina had not moved from Hampton Court Palace, she had travelled in her mind through the books she had read.

This had made her more intelligent and more perceptive than any woman he had ever known before.

"I have so much to show you, my darling," he said. "But not even the Taj Mahal, the Pyramids, or the Acropolis are more beautiful than you."

"And no Greek god, not even Apollo, could be more handsome than you," Zorina replied.

Rudolf laughed, and then he said:

"Go on thinking like that, for I shall be a very jealous husband. If I find you even looking at another man, I shall either strangle or beat you."

He spoke fiercely.

Zorina laughed:

"You will get very conceited, my darling, if I keep telling you how wonderful I think you are, and how, as far as I am concerned, no other man exists."

She paused and then went on:

"To me you are a god or a Knight in Shining Armour. You can take your choice."

It was with difficulty that Rudolf left her to collect more eggs, freshly baked bread, and other food from Frau Toger.

While he was away, Zorina tidied up the house, laid the table for dinner, and thought she had never been so happy in her whole life.

In fact, she had never known such happiness existed or how different everything seemed when one was in love.

As she made the bed, which had a soft mattress of goose feathers, she thought of Rudolf and the ecstasy he had given her.

She knew that nothing else could matter beside their love.

Zorina believed him when he said that he would never regret for one moment giving up being a Royal Prince.

Her own title had been of little importance when she

and her mother had been so poor at Hampton Court Palace.

But for Rudolf it was different.

He not only had the Palace as his home, but he had the respect and admiration of the Court as his background.

He also had his horses and servants to wait on him, whether he was staying at home or travelling abroad.

It was almost as if someone else rather than herself asked the question:

'Can I compensate him for losing so much?'

Then, as she patted the soft pillows on which their heads had lain side by side, Zorina knew the answer was "Yes."

The love they had for each other was the love for which God had created men and women and for which each one of them strove, whether knowingly or unknowingly.

Many failed ever to find it, but for those who, like themselves, had been so fortunate, it was a pearl beyond price.

They could only go down on their knees and pray that they would never lose anything so precious.

"I love you, darling," Zorina said, and kissed the place on the pillow where Rudolf's head had rested.

When she heard him coming back up the path, carrying a huge basket of food in one hand and a bag in the other, she ran to meet him.

She flung her arms around him and kissed him as if he had been away for years.

"You are back and I missed you," she cried. "Ten centuries have passed since you went away."

"Let me put the food down," Rudolf said, "so that I

can tell you how much I have missed you."

They kissed each other until Zorina said she was very hungry and they must start preparing their evening meal.

"Frau Toger feels insulted," Rudolf said, "because we have not wanted her help since we have been here. I told her that to-morrow, when we have gone out, she can come and clean the house."

He paused and then added:

"She can also bring us some more food to spare me from having to fetch it."

"I have cleaned and tidied the house myself," Zorina said. "I shall be offended if you think that I have not done it properly."

"I can see you have worked very hard," Rudolf replied. "Now I must pay your wages, which will be in kisses."

"I am very expensive," Zorina warned him.

He kisses her until once again they had to force themselves to remember they required something to eat.

They sat talking to each other over dinner, which they had finally prepared, until the sun sank behind the mountains and the first evening star flickered in the sky.

Zorina gave a little shiver, and Rudolf said:

"I must light the fires, my darling. It is getting cold, and you are inadequately clothed for the wind which blows down from the snow."

"I can wear my cape," Zorina replied.

"I think you would be warmer in bed," Rudolf said. "And then there is no need for me to light two fires."

"I believe you are just making an excuse for being lazy," Zorina teased him.

Then as he picked her up in his arms, she knew that

there was already a fire burning in his eyes and little flames were rising deep within her.

*　　*　　*

"What are we going to do today?" Zorina asked the next morning after she had insisted on preparing Rudolf's breakfast.

He had stood in the sunshine at the open door watching her.

As she came from the kitchen—her face a little flushed from the heat of the stove and her hair curling softly around her oval face—he thought it was impossible for any woman to be so lovely.

He knew that he was wildly and irrevocably in love.

She aroused in him emotions which were different from anything he had ever felt before.

He had vowed when they knelt in the little Church and the Cardinal had married them, that he would look after her and protect her all his life.

It was something he intended to do, and every moment he was with Zorina he felt his need of her growing and expanding.

It was not only her beauty but her intrinsic purity that made her so different from any woman he had ever known.

The sharpness and perceptiveness of her brain delighted him, as did the way she responded to everything he asked of her in the act of love.

But it was still more than that.

It was, he thought, that her soul spoke to his soul and spiritually they were as close, and a part of each other, as they were physically.

When Zorina had put the last dish down on the table, she said:

"Breakfast is ready."

Rudolf walked towards her and asked:

"Have I told you yet this morning how I love you?"

Her eyes shone and she turned towards him with an endearing little movement which touched his heart.

He moved his lips over the softness of her cheeks before he kissed her eyes, her straight little nose, and then her lips.

He felt her quiver, and he said in a voice which suddenly deepened:

"I want you. Breakfast can wait."

Zorina gave a little cry:

"You are not to spoil it, when I have taken so much trouble!"

She moved away from him and sat down to pour out his coffee.

Rudolf smiled as he said:

"Are you refusing me—for the first time—and also disobeying me?"

"I am trying to make you behave sensibly!"

"If you want me to be sensible, you will have to hide your face and conceal your lips."

Rudolf paused, and then went on:

"I will definitely borrow one of Frau Toger's shawls and hand-knitted skirts for you to wear!"

Zorina laughed.

"You will have to buy me something very soon or that is exactly what I shall need."

"We will talk about it this afternoon. I am so happy here, I cannot bear to leave."

"And I feel the same," Zorina said, putting out her

hand. "Oh, darling, what do clothes matter? Let us stay here as long as we can in our own wonderful little Paradise."

Rudolf kissed her hand and then, for a moment, they just looked at each other, before he said very quietly:

"I worship you."

*　　*　　*

They left the table, when they had finished, to be cleared away by Frau Toger and went out into the sunshine.

"I think what we will do, if you can manage it," Rudolf said, "is to climb a little way up the mountain."

"That is what I would love to do," Zorina replied.

"The view is even more breathtaking than it is from here. You can look over almost the whole of Leothia."

Zorina thought that perhaps it would be Rudolf's way of saying good-bye to the country to which he belonged.

She did not speak of it aloud, she merely said:

"I shall have to come just as I am. If I get very sunburnt without a hat, you will still have to go on loving me!"

"Bring your chiffon scarf," Rudolf replied. "I do not want you to spoil your skin."

She smiled at him and then, as she turned to go back into the house to fetch her scarf, she looked down towards the valley and was suddenly very still.

Coming up the path she could see, moving through the trees, there were men on horses.

Zorina gave a gasp of horror and moved towards where Rudolf was standing at the edge of the stream.

Before she reached him he knew from the expression on her face that something was wrong.

"What is it, my darling?" he asked.

"They have . . . found us . . . oh . . . Rudolf, they have . . . found us! Where . . . can we . . . hide?"

He looked downwards as she had done.

There were at least six men on horseback coming up the twisted path towards them.

Rudolf drew Zorina into the house.

He walked into the bed-room and she saw him take from the drawer, where she had tidied it away, his tie, and put it round his neck.

She realised that he intended to receive their unwanted guests looking dignified.

She ran to the cupboard to fetch his coat and put it down beside him.

Then she went to the mirror to tidy her hair, knowing it was not fashionably arranged as it had been when she left the Palace.

Because it was long and thick, she merely twisted it into a chignon at the back of her head and pinned it as securely as possible with the few hairpins she had left.

Rudolf shrugged himself into his coat and, putting his arms around Zorina, said quietly:

"Do not be afraid, my darling."

"They will . . . not take . . . me away from . . . you?" she asked in a frightened voice.

"You are my wife—whatever happens, that is irrevocable."

"You . . . are sure . . . quite sure?" Zorina asked.

Now the fear in her voice was very apparent.

"You must trust me."

He kissed her very gently and felt her trembling against him.

She did not speak, she did not say it aloud, but he

knew what Zorina was thinking. That if they were separated, she would die.

He knew, too, that there would be no point for either of them in going on living without the other.

Holding his head high and looking, although he was not aware of it, very regal, Rudolf drew Zorina out of the bed-room and into the Sitting-Room.

The sunshine was coming through the windows but Zorina felt that everything was dark.

She was being carried away from the dazzling light of the mountains of love into a valley of despair.

They heard the sound of the first horse stepping onto the plateau on which the house was built.

Rudolf did not move.

They stood together, side by side, with their backs to the chimney-piece—waiting.

There were voices and then footsteps, and finally in through the open door there came the Lord Chamberlain.

Rudolf's fingers tightened on Zorina's hand.

Her heart was beating frantically and she was trying to stop herself from trembling.

At the same time, if he could hold his head high, then she could do the same.

Only her eyes revealed the fear that was seeping through her.

The Lord Chamberlain stood for a moment looking at them both, and then unexpectedly he smiled before he bowed his head.

"Good morning, Sire," he said. "I am gratified to find that I was correct in thinking you would be here."

He moved forward as he spoke.

Then, as he stood in front of Rudolf, he unexpectedly went down on one knee.

"The King is dead," he said in a firm tone. "Long live the King!"

For a moment Rudolf seemed turned to stone and Zorina did not understand.

Then, as the Lord Chamberlain rose to his feet, he said:

"I bring you, Sire, the sad tidings of yesterday."

He paused and then continued:

"His Majesty, accompanied by the Crown Prince, drove in State to the Houses of Parliament. An anarchist threw a bomb into the open carriage."

He paused again, but as both Rudolf and Zorina were incapable of speaking, he went on:

"The anarchist was shot by the soldiers on duty, but it was too late to save the King or Prince Karl. I can, therefore, only ask you, Sire, to return to the Palace and take up your new position."

"It is difficult to comprehend that this has happened," Rudolf said in a low voice. "It is a tremendous shock, as you can imagine."

The Lord Chamberlain replied:

"We all understand, Sire, but your presence is vitally needed."

"I realise that," Rudolf said. "But if I return as you ask, I must bring my wife with me."

Zorina expected the Lord Chamberlain to look shocked and astonished, instead of which he said:

"I will be honest with Your Majesty and say that is what I thought must have happened when I learnt you were both missing."

"What I would really like to know," Rudolf said, "is how you had any idea we might be here."

The Lord Chamberlain gave a little laugh.

"I congratulate myself, Sire, on being a good detective."

"It is certainly something I never expected you to be, My Lord."

"I looked for a clue," the Lord Chamberlain explained, "in Your Majesty's private desk at the Palace."

As if he thought Rudolf might be angry, the Lord Chamberlain went on hastily:

"I know Your Majesty will understand that I had to act quickly. There was no one to take command and everything was in a turmoil following the assassination."

"What did you find in my desk?" Rudolf enquired.

"A letter from your friend, Bernard, telling you that he was going to Greece and saying that his house was at your disposal if you wished to use it."

Rudolf laughed.

"So it was as easy as that!"

"I know the girl to whom Bernard is engaged, and her father is an old friend of mine."

The Lord Chamberlain paused, then went on:

"He had often discussed with me his anxiety about his daughter moving from their luxurious Castle into such a small home. Although I can see that it is, in its way, very attractive."

"That is what my wife and I have found," remarked Rudolf.

There was the sound of a horse shaking its bridle outside, and the Lord Chamberlain said:

"Please, Your Majesty, come back and help us. There

is something like a panic at the moment in Archam."

He spoke pleadingly as he continued:

"When the people know you are back and have taken over the Throne, the impending Coronation will prevent them from dwelling on the horrors of what has just occurred."

Zorina could understand exactly what he implied. She looked up at Rudolf and knew that he was aware of it too.

"We will come back with you," Rudolf said with the emphasis on the first word.

The Lord Chamberlain hesitated.

"Perhaps, Your Majesty, it would be wise to let people think that you have been staying with friends, and if Her Royal Highness returned to England for three months—".

"No!"

The monosyllable interrupting the Lord Chamberlain seemed to ring around the small room.

"I know what you are trying to say," Rudolf went on, "but I will have none of it."

Zorina turned towards him and, raising her head, said in a whisper:

"Perhaps . . . he is . . . right and it . . . would be best . . . for you."

"No," Rudolf said again. "We will return together and we shall tell the truth."

Both the Lord Chamberlain and Zorina looked at him in astonishment.

"The . . . truth?" Zorina questioned.

Rudolf looked down at her and she saw to her surprise that there was a twinkle in his eyes.

"All the world, and certainly the people of Leothia,

enjoy a love story, and ours will give them something to talk about!"

He saw that Zorina still did not understand, and he went on:

"We fell in love with each other, my darling, when I was in England."

He hesitated, as if feeling for words before he continued:

"Because you thought you must obey Queen Victoria and marry the King of Leothia, you came here with the intention of carrying out what had been asked of you, only to find, as I did, that love was stronger than duty, prestige, or a Throne."

Zorina could not take her eyes from him, and she was aware that the Lord Chamberlain was listening intently as Rudolf went on:

"We ran away after we had been married by Father Augustine, who was once the Cardinal of Archam, determined to give up our Royal rank and live together just as an ordinary married couple."

The Lord Chamberlain gave a little exclamation, but he did not interrupt, and Rudolf went on:

"The people will understand that because they need us, my wife and I are giving up not only our honeymoon but our plans to live quietly and incognito."

His voice rose a little as he said:

"In fact, we are making great sacrifices for our country. I know, when they hear the whole story, everyone will understand and appreciate it."

He went on:

"I can imagine nothing more calculated to take their minds off the horror of what has just occurred than that a Coronation should take place as soon as possible."

There was a note of laughter in Rudolf's voice as he ended:

"After all, Her Royal Highness Princess Zorina was sent by Queen Victoria to marry the King of Leothia, and that is exactly what she had done!"

"Oh . . . Rudolf . . . you are so . . . clever."

There were tears in Zorina's eyes as she whispered the words.

The Lord Chamberlain laughed before he said:

"May I say, most respectfully, Sire, that you are exactly the sort of King who is needed at this moment in Leothia."

He looked at Zorina and added:

"And no country, Ma'am, could have a more beautiful Queen."

"I think now," Rudolf said, "you should bring in the other Gentlemen you have with you, My Lord. My wife and I will offer them what refreshment is available."

The Lord Chamberlain bowed, then backed respectfully towards the door.

As he disappeared, Rudolf put his arms around Zorina.

"We have won, my darling! We have won!" he cried. "How could anyone have imagined in their wildest dreams that our fairy-story would end like this?"

Tears were running down Zorina's cheeks, but she whispered:

"You will be the most . . . handsome King in the . . . whole of . . . Europe."

Rudolf laughed as he kissed her.

Then they heard footsteps outside and she hastily moved away from him.

There was, fortunately, wine in the cupboard, as well

as coffee which Zorina made for the Gentlemen-in-Waiting who had accompanied the Lord Chamberlain.

They had brought with them two spare horses.

As one had a side-saddle, Zorina realised that the Lord Chamberlain had been remarkably perceptive and astute.

Only when she was alone with Rudolf for a moment in the beautifully decorated bed-room where they had slept for two unforgettable nights did she say:

"I am glad ... my darling ... that you will not ... have to ... leave your own country and that you will reign ... over it."

She hesitated, and then whispered:

"At the same time, I am ... afraid of leaving our ... happiness behind in this ... enchanted place."

"We will take our enchantment with us," Rudolf said. "We will also come back here again."

"When?"

"The moment I can get away," Rudolf replied. "After all, even a King is entitled to a honeymoon."

"Can we really do ... that?" Zorina enquired.

"If I am a King," Rudolf laughed, "I intend to have my own way. And nobody, not even my wife, shall stop me."

He kissed Zorina until the bed-room, with its carvings and white rugs and the sunshine coming through the blue-curtained windows, seemed to whirl dizzily around her.

She could feel her heart beating against his. She knew that once again he wanted to make love to her.

"Darling ... they are ... waiting for ... us," she whispered.

"I would like to make them wait," he answered.

His voice was deep and a little unsteady.

"We . . . must . . . go."

Reluctantly he took his arms from her.

Then, as she wrapped her chiffon scarf over her head, he took her cloak from the cupboard and, as it was too hot for her to wear it, carried it.

The horses were waiting, but Rudolf would let no one else lift Zorina into the saddle.

As they rode down the steep, twisting path between the trees, she looked back and thought perhaps she was leaving her happiness behind her.

Then, as they reached the valley and Rudolf was by her side, she knew that nothing mattered except that they were together.

There would be difficulties, there would be problems, there would undoubtedly be times of apprehension, but love would conquer them all.

The road widened and now she could see the roofs of Archam and, high above the City, white and beautiful against the blue sky, there was the Palace.

It seemed impossible to believe that she was going back—to a place she had left in the depths of utter despair to die—but now feeling very different.

She knew that Rudolf would do everything that Britain wanted from the King of Leothia.

He would strengthen the country and thus help to preserve the Balance of Power in Europe.

Above all, he would love her.

Their love was too great to be questioned or changed wherever they went or whatever they did.

She was thinking of this as Rudolf turned and looked at her.

Riding a superbly bred horse and wearing her white

165

gown with her chiffon scarf, she looked like an enchanted goddess who had stepped down from Olympus.

Their eyes met and Rudolf said, so that no-one else should hear:

"I adore you, my perfect, wonderful little bride. This is a new adventure we are starting together."

The way he spoke told her that was exactly what it was.

Zorina felt her heart leap towards him.

As her spirits rose, she laughed with sheer exhilaration because everything seemed dazzlingly exciting.

"An adventure," she repeated, "an adventure of love."

Then, as they rode on and she knew that Rudolf was as excited as she was, she was thanking God for all he had given them.

She was also praying that she and her beloved husband would have sons—several sons to ensure the succession of the monarchy of Leothia.

ABOUT THE AUTHOR

Barbara Cartland, the world's most famous romantic novelist, who is also an historian, playwright, lecturer, political speaker and television personality, has now written over 500 books and sold over 450 million books the world over.

She has also had many historical works published and has written four autobiographies as well as the biographies of her mother and that of her brother, Ronald Cartland, who was the first Member of Parliament to be killed in the last war. This book has a preface by Sir Winston Churchill and has just been republished with an introduction by Sir Arthur Bryant.

Love at the Helm, a novel written with the help and inspiration of the late Admiral of the Fleet, the Earl Mountbatten of Burma, is being sold for the Mountbatten Memorial Trust.

Miss Cartland in 1978 sang an Album of Love Songs with the Royal Philharmonic Orchestra.

In 1976 by writing twenty-one books, she broke the world record and has continued for the following nine years with twenty-four, twenty, twenty-three, twenty-four, twenty-four, twenty-five, twenty-three, twenty-six, and twenty-two. She is in the *Guinness Book of Records* as the best-selling author in the world.

She is unique in that she was one and two in the Dalton List of Best Sellers, and one week had four books in the top twenty.

In private life Barbara Cartland, who is a Dame of the Order of St. John of Jerusalem, Chairman of the St. John Council in Hertfordshire and Deputy President of the St. John Ambulance Brigade, has also fought for better conditions and salaries for Midwives and Nurses.

Barbara Cartland is deeply interested in Vitamin Therapy and is President of the British National Association for Health. Her book *The Magic of Honey* has sold throughout the world and is translated into many languages. Her designs "Decorating with Love" are being sold all over the U.S.A., and the National Home Fashions League named her in 1981, "Woman of Achievement."

In 1984 she received at Kennedy Airport America's Bishop Wright Air Industry Award for her contribution to the development of aviation; in 1931 she and two R.A.F. Officers thought of, and carried, the first aeroplane-towed glider air-mail.

Barbara Cartland's Romances (a book of cartoons) has been published in Great Britain and the U.S.A., as well as a cookery book, *The Romance of Food*, and *Getting Older, Growing Younger*. She has recently written a children's pop-up picture book, entitled *Princess to the Rescue*.

In January 1988 she received "La Médaille de Vermeil de la ville de Paris." This is the highest award to be given in France by the City of Paris.